DATE DUE

FE 27 '07	AP 20 11		
AP 06 '07	MY 07 12		
AP 24 '07	AP 05 13		
NO 14 '07	AP 3 13		
NO 27 07			
DE 11 07			
JA 23 08			
FE 15 08			
MR 24 08			
SE 30 08			
OC 17 08			
NO 26 08			
FE 12 09			
MR 03 09			
SE 21 09			
09			

The Case of
the Measled Cowboy

The Case of
the Measled Cowboy

John R. Erickson

Illustrations by Gerald L. Holmes

Viking

VIKING
Published by the Penguin Group
Penguin Putnam Books for Young Readers,
345 Hudson Street, New York, New York 10014, U.S.A.
Penguin Books Ltd, 27 Wrights Lane, London W8 5TZ, England
Penguin Books Australia Ltd, Ringwood, Victoria, Australia
Penguin Books Canada Ltd, 10 Alcorn Avenue,
Toronto, Ontario, Canada M4V 3B2
Penguin Books (N.Z.) Ltd, 182-190 Wairau Road, Auckland 10, New Zealand

Penguin Books Ltd, Registered Offices: Harmondsworth,
Middlesex, England

Published simultaneously by Viking and Puffin Books, members of Penguin
Putnam Books for Young Readers, 1999

1 3 5 7 9 10 8 6 4 2

LIBRARY OF CONGRESS CATALOGING-IN-PUBLICATION DATA
Erickson, John R., date
The case of the measled cowboy / by John R. Erickson ;
illustrations by Gerald L. Holmes.
p. cm. — (Hank the Cowdog ; 33)
Summary: When Slim is left to take care of the ranch and little
Alfred, who has the measles, he gets sick himself and a freak blizzard sets in,
so it is up to Hank to try to keep things under
control.
ISBN 0-670-88489-8 (Viking).—ISBN 0-14-130423-5 (Puffin)
[1. Dogs—Fiction. 2. Ranch life—Fiction. 3. Measles—Fiction.
4. Humorous stories.] I. Holmes, Gerald L., ill. II. Title.
III. Series: Erickson, John R., date Hank the Cowdog ; 33.
PZ7.E72556Catt 1999 [Fic]—dc21 98-41787 CIP AC

Printed in the United States of America
Set in New Century Schoolbook

CONTENTS

The Case of
the Measled Cowboy

Strange Things Afoot on the Ranch

It's me again, Hank the Cowdog. It all began in the fall of the year. November. Yes, it was November, a day or two after Thanksgiving.

Thanksgiving always comes in November. I don't know why, but it does.

Drover and I were standing near the yard gate. All at once the back door of the ranch house flew open and out came Loper. He breezed through the gate and didn't even bother to speak to us. He seemed deep in thought. Preoccupied. In a hurry.

He went up the hill to the machine shed, opened the west door, and backed Sally May's car out of the shed. This was odd. Loper seldom drove Sally May's car.

I turned to my assistant. "Drover, something's going on around here."

He gave me that goofy smile of his. "Yeah, and aren't we glad? Gosh, if nothing went on, nothing would ever happen and that would be pretty boring."

"I think you missed the point. The point is that something highly unusual and out of the ordinary is about to happen. Would you care to hear the evidence?"

"Oh . . . not really. I'm kind of busy right now."

I glared at the runt. "Busy? You're just sitting there."

"Yeah, but I'm watching the clouds, and they keep moving around. About the time I get one cloud watched, it moves away and another one comes along, so I have to keep watching. It sure keeps me busy."

"Oh brother."

"What do you reckon clouds are made of?"

"They're made of . . . how should I know what clouds are made of?"

"I thought you knew just about everything."

"You thought . . . hmmmm. Good point, Drover. I mean, I've never pretended to know everything about everything, but I do know quite a lot about many things."

2

"That's what I meant."

"Oh. Well, in that case, I guess we can take some time out of our busy schedules for a few questions. Fire away."

"Oh good. I wonder what clouds are made of."

"That's not a question, Drover, it's a statement. I can't give an answer to a statement."

"I wonder why."

"That's another statement and I can't answer it either. If you want an answer, ask a question."

"Okay. How long's a piece of string?"

"Two feet."

"How about a centipede?"

"One foot."

He turned to me and twisted his head around. "I thought a centipede had a whole bunch of feet."

"A centipede has a whole bunch of feet, Drover, but is only one foot long. You see, the word 'centipede' is made up of two parts: 'centi' and 'pede.'"

"I peed on an electric fence one time."

"'Don't interrupt."

"It sure woke me up."

"Hush. 'Centi' comes from the root word 'cent,' and a cent is one penny. Therefore, it follows from simple logic that a centipede is only one foot long."

"I'll be derned. How does he walk on one foot?"

"I didn't say he had only one foot. I said he was only one foot long."

"Boy, what a miracle. All those legs and only one foot."

I gave him a withering glare. "Drover, sometimes I get the feeling that you're not paying attention."

"Yeah, I keep watching the clouds, but that gets kind of boring."

"Then why do you keep watching them?"

"I don't know. Can't think of anything else to do . . . I guess."

I marched several steps away and tried to clear the vapors out of my head. "Drover, sometimes I feel you're trying to lead me into a state of chaos."

"I thought it was Texas."

"Please don't say another word."

"Okay."

I stared at him in disbelief. "You just said another word."

"I did? Gosh, I didn't hear a thing. Maybe I've got some wax in this ear." He sat down and began scratching his left ear with his left hind leg. "No, the ear's okay, but this leg's killing me."

"We should be so lucky."

"What?"

"I said, nothing's wrong with your leg. You're a hypodermiac, that's all, and you're about to drive me batty."

"Yeah, and Loper's driving Sally May's car out of the machine shed. Something must be going on around here, 'cause he doesn't drive her car unless they're going on a trip."

I cut my eyes from side to side. Somehow the little moron had brought this senseless conversation right back where it had started, and had even managed to point out the first important clue in the case—a clue I had observed and had been trying to mention, only he had pulled me into the swamp of his blabbering.

I don't know how he does it.

He's the weirdest little mutt I ever knew.

And it really burned me up that he'd stolen my clue, but I didn't have much time to think about it because at that very moment, Loper swung the car into the gravel drive. I was just sitting there, minding my own business and trying to recover from Drover's latest assault on my mental health, and . . .

Loper blew the horn and stuck his head out the window. "Get out of the way! We've got places to go and you're sitting in the way of progress."

Fine. I could take a hint, but he didn't need to screech at me and blow the horn.

Dogs have feelings too.

I moved, but not before he blew the horn again. That really wasn't necessary, but when he gets in a hurry . . . oh well.

He jumped out of the car and dashed into the house. Hmm, very strange. It appeared that someone was fixing to leave on a trip. The evidence was certainly stacking up that way.

I took this opportunity to do a quick Wash and Clean on the car tires. They were pretty dusty and needed to be shined up. That done, I drifted back to the yard gate to watch the loading operation. Slim had come up from the corrals by then and was leaning against the car, cleaning his fingernails with a pocket knife.

Have I pointed out that Slim always seems to be *leaning* against something or other? It's true. Once his legs quit moving, he just naturally slumps against whatever is handy—a post, a tree, the side of a building, or a car. It's no big deal, I suppose, but it's the kind of detail a Head of Ranch Security is likely to notice.

You never see us dogs leaning against things.

He was leaning against the car. I went over to him and sat down. I gave him Friendly Wags and he said, "Howdy, pooch."

At that very moment the back door burst open and Loper staggered out, loaded down with suitcases, Molly's diaper bag, and Molly's high chair. The expression on his face would have caused a grizzly bear to run. His brow had formed a maze of wrinkles. His eyes were bulging out and that big vein in the middle of his forehead was showing.

He saw Slim. "Hey! Would it be too much trouble for you to open the gate?"

Slim looked up from his fingernail business and grinned. "Y'all moving?" He put away his knife and opened the gate. With all this baggage, Loper didn't quite fit through the opening of the gate, but he managed to smash his way through, causing things to scrape and snap.

"Thanks. How about the car door? I know you're busy, but maybe you could work that into your schedule."

Slim opened the back door. "Shore. Be glad to, you being so sweet and everything."

Loper pitched the stuff inside. "How can one woman and one baby need so much junk? Do you think we're going on an ocean cruise for a month? No! This is for two days in Abilene! And this is only half of it. I've still got another load."

Slim nodded and tried to bite back his smile. "Anything I can do to help?"

"Sure. You go to Abilene and let me stay at the ranch where I belong."

"Gosh, I wish I could."

Loper stabbed him with a pair of ice pick eyes. "You're enjoying this, aren't you?"

"No, I hate to see a fellow cowboy suffer."

"Ha! The Lord loves a cheerful liar." He glanced at his watch. "We should have been on the road thirty minutes ago." Shaking his head and muttering under his breath, he stalked back into the house.

Instantly, and I mean immediately, Slim slumped against the car and fished a toothpick out of his shirt pocket. "He sure gets gripey, don't he? I can't imagine why his in-laws would want him around. I'll be glad to be rid of him for a couple of days." He took a big yawn and stretch. "I plan to have me a nice restful holiday, pooch."

The back door flew open and out came Loper again, loaded down with more bags and suitcases. He struggled down the sidewalk and yelled for Slim to open the gate for him. Slim did, at his usual speed.

"Now, get the keys and unlock the trunk, would you?" Slim did, again at his usual speed. Loper stood there, holding all the bags and watching Slim move in slow motion. He gave his head a shake. "Slim, Abilene's going to be in ruins before you get the dadgum trunk unlocked. Would you hurry?"

Slim nodded and came around to the rear of the car. He held up the key ring, which had about fifteen keys on it. He tried one and it didn't work. He tried another and it didn't work. When the third key didn't work, Loper dropped the bags and trotted back to the house.

"You load the trunk and I'll see if I can get that woman out of the house."

The door slammed. Slim shifted his toothpick over to the other side of his mouth and looked down at me. "Well, there ain't but one key that'll open the trunk, and I don't figger he'd want me to use a can opener. Everything takes time."

Just then the back door flew open again and Loper stepped out on the porch. He looked up at the sky, took off his hat and fanned his face, and heaved a deep sigh.

"Never mind the trunk, Slim. The trip's been called off."

CHAPTER TWO

Little Alfred
Has Measles

L oper came out to the gate and joined us. "Alfred's got some red spots on his chest. He doesn't act sick but Sally May thinks he's coming down with measles. She doesn't think he ought to expose all the kinfolks."

Slim nodded. "Can you get someone to stay with him?"

"No. Too late. We'll just stay here."

"Well, you don't act very happy about it. Five minutes ago you were mad 'cause you had to leave. Now you're mad 'cause you can't."

Loper studied him for a moment. "Slim, you have no idea how life is lived in the Real World. All you bachelors have to do is decide which kind of jelly you want on your peanut butter sandwich."

"Well, I like jelly. And it's good for you. I read an article in the *Picayune* that said grape jelly is better for you than a trainload of lettuce leaves."

"That's baloney."

"Well now, they said baloney was high in vitamins too. That was one of the best articles I ever read."

Loper shook his head. "Look, I didn't want to go on this trip, but once the plans were made and the bags were packed, I was ready get on with it. Now she thinks Alfred's got measles. I don't know whether I'm coming or going."

"That's too bad. I was looking forward to some peace and quiet, once I got you off the place."

"Well, you can forget that. If I have to stay home, we're going to get some work done around here."

Slim nodded and looked at the sky. "Course, I guess Alfred could stay with me."

Loper's eyes came up. "You?" He laughed. "*You?*"

"What's so funny about that?"

"Well, for starters, my wife would never go for it. Leave her darling boy with a cowboy who can't even boil water?"

"I can too boil water. I do it every morning to make my coffee."

"So what would you feed him? Coffee grounds and peanut butter sandwiches?"

"You might be surprised, Loper. There's several things I know how to cook."

"Such as?"

"Such as . . . hamburger steak, chicken-fried steak, ham and eggs, and boiled turkey necks."

Loper gave him a long look. "You can cook all that?"

"Heck yeah, when I have to. Most generally I don't go to the trouble, but that don't mean I can't. You ought to try my boiled turkey necks sometime. You'd be a whole lot more respectful of my cookin' if you did."

Loper was deep in thought. He pushed his hat down to his nose and scratched the back of his head. "You know, that just might work."

"You bet. They're delicious."

"I'm talking about you keeping Alfred so we can get on with this trip. I mean, he doesn't look sick to me, just got some red spots." He thought about it some more. "Let me go consult with the lady of the house and see what she thinks."

He started toward the house and met Sally May at the back door. They discussed it in low voices. I didn't hear all that was said, but I did manage to pick up a line here and there. It appeared to me that Sally May didn't go for the idea at first, but Loper convinced her that it would be all right to leave for a couple of days.

Anyways, after a short conference, they both came down the sidewalk to talk it over with Slim. When he saw the hawkeyed look on Sally May's face, he stopped slouching and stood up straight. She got right to the point.

"Slim, I'll be honest. The thought of leaving Alfred with you makes me uneasy."

"Yes ma'am, I can understand that."

"On the other hand, he's not running a fever and he says he doesn't feel bad, so maybe . . . I'd hate to miss seeing my folks. This is their fortieth anniversary."

Slim nodded. "I'll be derned."

"All the family is going to be there."

"Uh-huh."

Loper stepped in. "Hon, if he has any problems, he can call. We'll turn around and come right back. But if we're going, we need to get on the road."

Sally May crossed her arms in front of her and thought about it. "Oh . . . I guess it might be all right."

"Great!" Loper headed for the car. "Let's load 'em up and move 'em out."

Sally May didn't move. She spent the next five minutes going over Rules and Regulations with

Slim, while Loper jingled the coins in his pockets and grabbed glances at his watch. Most of the rules had to do with Slim's taking Little Alfred's temperature, feeding him "nourishing, balanced meals," and making him brush his teeth, but then she came to what she called the "Tenth Commandment": *No dogs in the yard or in the house.*

Slim chuckled at that. "Heck, Sally May, you sure don't need to tell me that. No sir, as long as old Slim Chance is in charge of things, we'll keep our furry friends outside where they belong . . . won't we, Hank?"

Huh? All at once they were looking at . . . well, at ME, you might say, and suddenly I felt . . .

"Don't you worry, Sally May. We'll take care of everything. Now you go and have yourself a good time, hear? If I have any problems, I'll give you a call."

"Well . . ." Her eyes darted from me to Slim and back to me. ". . . all right." She went back into the house to say good-bye to Alfred and to get Baby Molly.

Loper drifted over to where we were standing. He was shaking his head. "She's a wonderful woman, but I swear . . . traveling with her is an ordeal."

Slim grinned and nodded and said, "Yalp."

Loper shot him a glare. "That's right, you go ahead and enjoy this, buddy, but one of these days you'll find some sweet thing to marry, and I'm going to enjoy watching you."

At last Sally May came out of the house with Baby Molly. Loper made a dive to open the car door for her, but instead of getting in, she handed him the baby and rearranged all the luggage in the trunk and backseat. Loper's eyes almost bugged out of his head, but he didn't say anything.

Slim watched and grinned. He caught Loper's eye and gave him a little wave with two fingers. Loper ground his teeth and muttered words under his breath, until at last Sally May was ready to leave. Loper stuffed her into the car, handed her the baby, slammed the door, and trotted around to the driver's side.

His parting words to Slim were, "Try not to do anything stupid while I'm gone. I guess you've had the measles, haven't you?" He didn't wait for the answer. He leaped into the car and they roared away.

Slim waved good-bye. "Nope. Never had the measles, and don't plan to either."

The car turned left at the county road, flew over the cattle guard, and zoomed off to the west, leaving a plume of white caliche dust hanging in the air.

By this time Slim was slouching against the gate

post. "Boy, there ain't a breath of air this morning. The last time it was this still, we had a blizzard the next day. But it's too early in the season for that." He yawned. "Well, I'd better go check on the patient, and then I'm going to spend the next two days catching up on some of this work. You dogs can run the ranch. And remember what Loper said: don't do anything stupid. I know that'll be hard for y'all, but do your best, hear?"

What was *that* supposed to mean? Okay, maybe he was trying to be funny, but sometimes . . . oh well. On this outfit, part of a dog's job is ignoring most of what the people say.

He shuffled through the gate, up the sidewalk, and into the house, humming a tune under his breath. No sooner was he inside the house than I heard something rattling the bushes on the south side of the house. My ears shot up and I turned to my assistant.

"Did you hear that?"

Drover gave me his usual grin. "Oh yeah, I heard the whole thing."

"What do you make of it?"

"Well, I guess we can't do anything stupid for two whole days."

"Not that. I heard a sound coming from those bushes over there."

"I'll be derned."

We turned our respective eyes toward the alleged bushes and suddenly . . . holy smokes, a shock wave moved through my entire body and all the way out to the end of my tail, and I even heard a kind of gurgling bark work its way out of the inner depths of my throat.

You won't believe this, but right there in those bushes was crouched some kind of . . . some kind of *humanoid monster* . . . a midget monster with two arms and two legs, and he was wearing striped *prison clothes*! And he was grinning and waving at us and . . .

Well, you know me, fellers. When I see monsters and things lurking around the house, I don't just sit there looking simple. I bark. Yes siree, I ran backward three steps, raised the hair on the back of my back, and cut loose with a . . .

Hold it. Cancel the Code Three. Forget what I said about . . .

Okay, our latest intelligence reports had said that Little Alfred was sick, right? Sick with the measles and in bed, and so the last place we would have expected to find a sick child was in the bushes on the south side of the house, right? But guess who was in the bushes.

Alfred. He was wearing his striped pajamas.

And he sure didn't look sick to me. He waved a greeting and put his finger to his lips and said, "Shhhhh!" Okay, fine. We could shhhhh, but what was he doing out of his bed, out of the house, and hiding in the bushes? It seemed pretty strange to me.

But just then he answered my question. "I'm hiding fwom Swim."

Oh, so that was it. The little skunk was already playing games with his baby-sitter, and the dust from his parents' car had barely had time to settle. It appeared that old Slim might have bitten off more than he could bite.

Bitten off more than he could bark.

Bitten off more than . . . phooey.

All at once it appeared that old Slim might have his hands cut out for him, and I had a feeling that he wouldn't get much work done.

Yes sir, if Slim had known what adventures lay ahead, I don't think he ever would have let Loper and Sally May leave the ranch. I don't want to reveal too much about this case, but you'll never guess . . .

Better not say any more.

CHAPTER THREE

Red Spots on Slim

Well, it took Slim five minutes to figure out that Alfred was missing. He came out the back door and walked over to where Drover and I were standing. Sitting, actually. We had gotten tired of standing and had sat down beside the yard fence. Alfred was still hiding in the bushes, wearing a big devilish grin.

Slim walked up to us and stopped. I noticed that I was feeling just a bit . . . well, guilty, you might say. Not that we'd done anything wrong. We hadn't. We were as innocent as the driveled snow, but it just so happened that we knew where the guilty party was hiding.

Anyways, I was suddenly smitten by feelings of guilt and began whapping my tail on the ground.

These were Slow Whaps, the kind that are meant to express Deepest Concern and Purest Intentions. Drover must have been feeling guilty too, because he lowered his head and rolled over on his back.

Slim towered over us. He had a toothpick parked on one side of his mouth. I waited for him to accuse us of ... what? Hiding a crinimal? Contributing to the jailbreak of a minor? I didn't know what-all kinds of crimes we might be accused of, but I was pretty sure we would get blamed for something.

That's the way it usually turns out around here.

But you know what? He didn't say a word about Little Alfred. What he said was, "Well, dogs, let's load up some feed and go check them heifers."

And he started walking towards the pickup. I was shocked. I threw a glance over to the south side of the house and saw Little Alfred's face appear. His eyes were as big as coffee cups, and his mouth was hanging open. Oh, and that devilish little grin had vanished.

Slim opened the pickup door and whistled for us dogs to load up. Well ... I didn't feel good about leaving the boy, but we were being called to Active Duty and ... what's a dog supposed to do? We headed for the pickup and jumped into the cab.

Slim climbed in behind us and slammed the

door. He started the motor and put her in gear, and we began moving away from the house. We hadn't gone far when we heard screaming and yelling. We looked back toward the yard and saw the midget in prison stripes running in our direction. He was wearing big fluffy house shoes on his feet and he was waving his arms.

"Swim, Swim, don't weeve me!" Slim put on the brake and waited. Alfred ran up to the pickup. His face showed a high degree of shock, and maybe some fear also. Yes, the boy was pretty scared. "Were ya'll gonna weeve me here?"

Slim nodded. "Uh-huh, that's what we was fixing to do."

"You can't weeve me all by myself!"

"Why not? You left the place where you was supposed to be, so I figured you needed some time alone." Alfred shook his head and his lip began to tremble. "Here's the deal, son. I ain't going to chase you all over this ranch. Either you're sick or you ain't. Declare yourself and let's get on with it. If you're sick, get back in that bed and stay there. If you ain't sick, get in and let's go check heifers."

"Well . . . I don't feel sick."

"Then probably you ain't. Load up and let's go." He stepped out and Alfred joined us dogs on

the pickup seat. He didn't look near as cocky as he had about five minutes before, and that was the end of his playing Hide and Seek with Slim.

I must admit that I was impressed with the way Slim handled it. He may have been a bachelor, but he knew how to get the lad's attention. Don't argue, don't chase, just drive off.

We drove around to the feed barn and Slim got out and threw a sack of feed into the rear of the pickup. When he climbed back inside, Alfred said, "Hey Swim, can I dwive?"

Slim looked him over. "No."

"How come?"

"You ain't old enough. You've got to be six to drive a ranch pickup. You're only five."

"Pweeze."

"What if you got arrested and throwed in jail? In jail, they'd make you eat spinach three times a day. How would you like that?"

The boy narrowed his eyes. "Swim, you're teasing me."

"I am, huh? Well crawl over here and sit in my lap. I guess we've got nothing better to do."

Alfred crawled into Slim's lap and took the wheel. Slim let out the clutch and off we went to the Dutcher Creek pasture. Alfred "drove" all the way, and seemed right proud of himself.

When we got to the pasture, Slim turned off the key and blew the horn. As the heifers began coming up out of the creek, he took off his hat and fanned his face.

"Does it seem hot to y'all?" Alfred shook his head. "Boy, all at once I'm burning up." Slim took off his jacket and fanned his face again. I noticed that it looked a little red...his face, not his hat—his face looked red and he even had a few beads of sweat on the sides of his nose.

By then, the heifers had arrived. Slim got out

and poured the feed on the ground in a long line. We waited for him to join us in the cab, but he didn't, not for a while. Instead, he sat down on the back of the pickup bed and fanned his face again with his hat. At last he stepped down and walked around to the door. He had unbuttoned his shirt, and I noticed that his face had turned even redder than before.

"Boys, I don't know what's come over me, but all at once I ain't feeling so wonderful. I've got the sweats and I feel kindly weak. I sure hope this ain't a cold coming on."

"Maybe you're getting the measles."

Slim laughed. "Don't think so. Grown people don't get the measles. Measles and mumps is what they call 'children's diseases,' see, and by the time you get my age . . . good honk, now I'm cold." He put on his jacket and climbed into the cab. "Something ain't quite right here. Maybe we'd better go back to the house and I'll take me a little nap. I must be catching a sniffle."

"Hey Swim, you've got some wed spots on your face."

Slim gave the boy a hard stare. Then he looked at his face in the mirror. "Can't see a thing, mirror's too dirty, but I don't have any red spots."

Alfred shrugged. "Okay, Swim." Then he turned

to us dogs and whispered, "He's got wed spots."

I looked, and the boy was right. Hmmm.

Slim started the pickup and we drove back to the house. By the time we got there, he wasn't acting very perky. He kind of dragged his way toward the house, complaining that the sunlight was bothering his eyes. When he reached the yard gate, he stopped and leaned against the gate post.

He unsnapped all the buttons on his shirt. Alfred stared at his bare chest. "Hey Swim, you've got wed spots on your chest."

Slim looked. "That's a sure sign of a cold comin' on. All I need is a thirty-minute nap. And you're going to take one too."

"Aw Swim, can't I stay out here and pway wiff my doggies?"

"Negatory on that. I ain't fixing to close my eyes with you and them dogs running a-loose. Come on. When we get up from our naps, I'll make us a nice nourishing lunch."

"Oh good! How 'bout fwied chicken?"

"It's great stuff but it ain't one of my recipes. Makes too many dirty dishes. Think of something else."

"Okay. How about . . ."

"Better yet, let me give you the choices. We

can have vienna sausage or Chef Boy Howdy's canned spaghetti."

"Would you warm it up?"

"No. It dirties the pot. We can eat it out of the can, the cowboy way."

"Couldn't you wash the pot?"

"Too much trouble, and besides, I've got a cold. You ain't supposed to warsh pots when you've got a cold. Spreads germs." He started toward the back door. "So that settles it. When we get up from our naps, we'll have vienna sausage and crackers."

"And ketchup?"

"Okay, if you don't make a mess. I don't want your ma coming home to a dirty house. She already thinks I'm about half savage, and I don't need any more evidence against me. Come on."

Slim went into the house, wiping sweat from his forehead. Alfred waved good-bye to us dogs and said, "Y'all wait wight there. I'll be back after my dumb old nap."

He disappeared into the house, leaving Drover and me alone. I wasn't real excited at the prospect of spending any more time alone with Drover. I mean, he's a fairly nice little mutt in some ways, but also fairly boring.

As instructed, we sat down beside the yard gate. The minutes crawled by and after while, we found ourselves staring into each other's eyes.

"Drover, why are you staring at me?"

"Oh, I don't know. I ran out of things to do, I guess."

"Well, stare at something else. I don't enjoy being stared at."

"You stared at me first."

"I did not. I was merely looking. There's a big difference between staring and looking."

"I'll be derned. What's the difference?"

"The difference is . . . big. Huge."

"Yeah, but what is it?"

"If you don't know by now, Drover, I'm not going to waste my time telling you."

Silence. Then, "What should I stare at?"

"Anything but me. Just pick something out of the hat."

"I don't have a hat."

"I know you don't have a hat. You just barely have a head."

"I thought I had a pretty nice head. Now you're making fun of it."

"I'm not making fun of your head. The point is that your head is fairly empty."

"How'd you know that?"

I heaved a sigh. "Every time I look into your eyes, Drover, I see a vast emptiness."

F.
Fri

"No fooling?"

"Honest. You should try to look yourself in the eyes sometime."

"Gee, I never thought of that." You know what he did then? He crossed his eyes! And even more amazing, he seemed excited about it. "Gosh, this is fun. I never would have thought of doing this. Thanks, Hank."

I watched the little mutt for five whole minutes, cross-eyed and grinning. At last I could stand it no longer. "All right, that's enough. You're embarrassing me. If someone came along and saw us here, they'd know for sure that you're a goofball. And they might even think we were friends."

"Oh, I don't mind."

"I know *you* don't mind, but I do. I have my reputation to think about." He uncrossed his eyes and laid down. So did I. "The trouble with you, Drover, is that you take a good idea and run it into the ground."

"I thought the trouble with me was that my tail was too short."

"You have many troubles."

"Yeah, and this old leg of mine . . ."

"Drover, please hush and go to sleep. We'll discuss your troubles some other time. Good night."

"It's still daylight. And you know what else?

The wind just shifted to the north. And it feels kind of chilly. And clouds are moving in."

"Drover, for the last tork, snerk the honking watermelons and biffle the piffle . . . zzzzzzzz."

I must have dozed off. When I awoke, something strange had happened.

CHAPTER FOUR

Stormy Weather

Y ou're probably wondering what the strange-ness was that happened whilst I was ... whilst I was resting my eyes and restoring my precious bodily fluids. Well, several things.

First off, the weather changed grammatically. I mean, in that short span of half an hour or so, the day changed from bright fall to gloomy winter. Heavy gray clouds covered the sun and a sharp wind was slicing in from the north. Fellers, we had just been hit by an old-fashioned norther, and the temperature was falling like a gutted sparrow from the uppermost branches of the tree of ...

The temperature was falling like a rock, shall we say, and the wind was pushing puffs of dust and tumbleweeds ahead of it, moaning through the trees, and causing leaves to swirl and clatter across the ground.

I sat straight up and turned to ... whoever that was ... okay, it was Drover. Yes, of course, it was Drover, and I turned straight up and sat ... I sat straight up and turned to Drover and said, "Who's going on here and what's the porkchop of this?"

I noticed that he was shivering—a pretty important clue. "I don't know, but I'm cold."

"Why wasn't I called? Nobody cleared this with ..." I shook several vapors out of my head. "Okay, we've got a neither in progress, Nover."

"My name's Drover."

"Ah ha! Just as I subjected. They thought they could sneak a norther onto my ranch, they thought I wouldn't ..." I blinked my eyes several times. "Where are we?"

"Well, let's see." He rolled his eyes around. "Somewhere in Texas, I think."

"Yes, of course. How long have we been gone and how did we get here? I need facts, Drover, facts and details, for you see ... wait a minute. We took a little nap, didn't we?"

"Well, you did. I couldn't sleep."

"Objection! The witness is dealing in hearsay and gossip. The fact in this case is that you can't prove that I was actually asleep, isn't that correct?"

"Well . . . if you weren't asleep, how come you just woke up?"

I cut my eyes from side to side. Was this some kind of trick question? Just for a second it caught me off guard, but it didn't matter because at that very moment, the case went plunging into a new direction. I heard a sound behind me. I whirled around and saw . . .

Okay, it was Little Alfred. He'd just come out of the house, and suddenly the pieces of the puddle began falling to pieces. Puzzle. Do you see the meaning of this? If Little Alfred had just come out of the house, it meant that he . . . it didn't mean much of anything, actually, except that he'd finished his nap, and by then I was wide awake and alert. After a brief mutiny of my mental faculties, I had regained control of my ship.

I whirled back to Drover. "I must ask you to disregard everything I've said up to this point. My mind was in a confused state."

"Yeah, 'cause you were half-asleep."

I gave him a stern glare. "You keep saying that. What's your point? Are you trying to grind up an ax? Because if you are, let me remind you . . ." I wasn't able to finish my thought, for at that moment Little Alfred joined us.

"Hi, doggies. You waited for me, didn't you? Nice doggies."

Yeah, that was me, all right, a "nice doggie" who obeyed orders and did his best to please the people in the house. I turned to my little pal and gave him Welcoming Wags on the tail section. I noticed right away that he had changed out of his pajamas and was now wearing his usual ranch clothes: striped overalls, black boots, and a little wool jacket. This seemed a pretty strong clue that he wasn't sick anymore and that the measles hadn't done him much harm.

That was good news. But where was Slim? I kept expecting to see him come out the back door at any moment, but he didn't. We waited and waited. At last Alfred addressed the matter.

"You know what? Swim's sick. He's in bed and won't get up. And you know what else?" The boy drew closer and dropped his voice to a whisper. "He's got gobs of wed spots on his face, and I think he's got my measles!"

I turned to Drover. "Did you hear that?"

His eyes were blank. "Hear what?"

"What Alfred just said."

"Oh yeah. Somebody's swimming in bed, and then they're going to have a measly wedding. I think that's what he said."

"That's NOT what he said. You garbled the entire message and turned it into sheer garbage. What would you do if I weren't around, Drover?"

"Oh, I don't know. Sleep, most likely. I never seem to get enough sleep."

"Ha. You get enough sleep for fifteen dogs. That's all you ever do, and if I weren't around to force you out of bed once in a while, you'd turn into . . . I don't know what. Yes I do. You'd turn into a bedbug with bed sores, and how would you like that?"

"Well, I love sleep but I've never cared for bugs. Especially scorpions. I got stung on the nose one time. Sure did hurt."

I glared at the runt. "Do you want to hear the message or not? If you'll pay attention for just a minute, I'll translate it from Kid Language into our native tongue."

"Yeah, I almost forgot about that."

"Forgot about what?"

"The time I tried to eat a wasp and he bit me on the tongue."

"Wasps don't bite. They sting."

"Yeah, it stung like fire, and that was the last time I ever tried to eat a wasp."

I stared at him for a long moment of heartbeats. My lips moved but no words came out. I just couldn't think of any words to describe . . . oh well. I turned away from the little lunatic and tried to get on with my life.

Alfred had assumed a thoughtful pose. I wondered what he was being so thoughtful about, and I soon found out. He said, "You know what, doggies? I think we need to help Swim."

Help Slim? My mind raced back through the molasses swamp of the last several minutes and . . . oh yes, Slim. We'd been talking about Slim. He was inside the house, ill with something.

We needed to help Slim? Well, that sounded like a good and decent thing to do. I'd always been the kind of dog who was ready and eager to help the less fortunate in this old world, and yes, by George, if Slim was sick and disfortunate, maybe we should help him.

But how? I waited to hear the rest of it.

Alfred arched his brows. "Why don't we go inside?"

Inside? *Inside the house?* Hey, I didn't want to throw cold water on Alfred's parade, but the very thought of entering Sally May's . . .

"See, my mom's gone."

Yes, that was true.

"And it's cold out here."

Yes, true again. However . . .

"And we have to go inside to help Swim."

Hmm. Good point. In fact, three good points, all in a row, and the very best one was the first: Sally May was gone. Heh heh. Yes, of course, it was all fitting together. Into the house and out again, no messes, no clues, no evidence of the . . . uh . . . of our brief occupation of the, uh, house, shall we say. Warm house, soft carpet upon which to lie, perhaps a few scraps from the, uh, family's huge supply of . . .

Great idea! But of course what made it even greater and more noble was the fact that we would be HELPING SLIM IN HIS HOUR OF NEED. The poor guy was sick! My heart went out to him, and I knew that if Sally May were present, she would *want* us to help the sick and the needy of this world. And if we didn't, if we followed our own selfish desires, if we neglected our friend Slim . . . why, she would be shocked and disappointed.

Alfred was right. We had a heavy responsibility here. It was our duty to care for Slim and nurse him back to health, and by George, I was ready to volunteer for the job. Sure, I had other work to do, jobs lined up, patrols to make, reports to file, but if a guy's too busy to help out the widows and shut-ins, he's just too busy.

I managed to express all of this to Alfred,

mostly through wags and Expressions of Deep Concern. I was ready to help our friend, our dear friend, our poor dear sick friend. Alfred gave me a grin and a wink, and opened the yard gate.

I went into the yard. Just for an instant, I felt . . . well, a little uneasy. I mean, old habits die hardly . . . old habits hardly die . . . old habits . . . phooey. Sally May was gone and I knew she wouldn't be back for two days, and what she didn't know wouldn't . . .

I marched straight over to that big shrub beside the porch and gave it a squirt. There! By George, I'd been wanting to do that for years. I was in the process of scratching up some grass when who or whom do you suppose stuck his head out of the flower bed?

Pete.

Kitty Kitty.

He beamed me a sour smile. "Ummmm! I saw what you did, Hankie, and it wasn't very nice."

"Oh yeah?"

"That's right. Sally May wouldn't approve. You know how she feels about dogs in the yard."

I laughed in his face. "Hey Kitty, I've got some bad news for you. Sally May's gone for the day and we dogs are taking over the yard. Do you know what that means?"

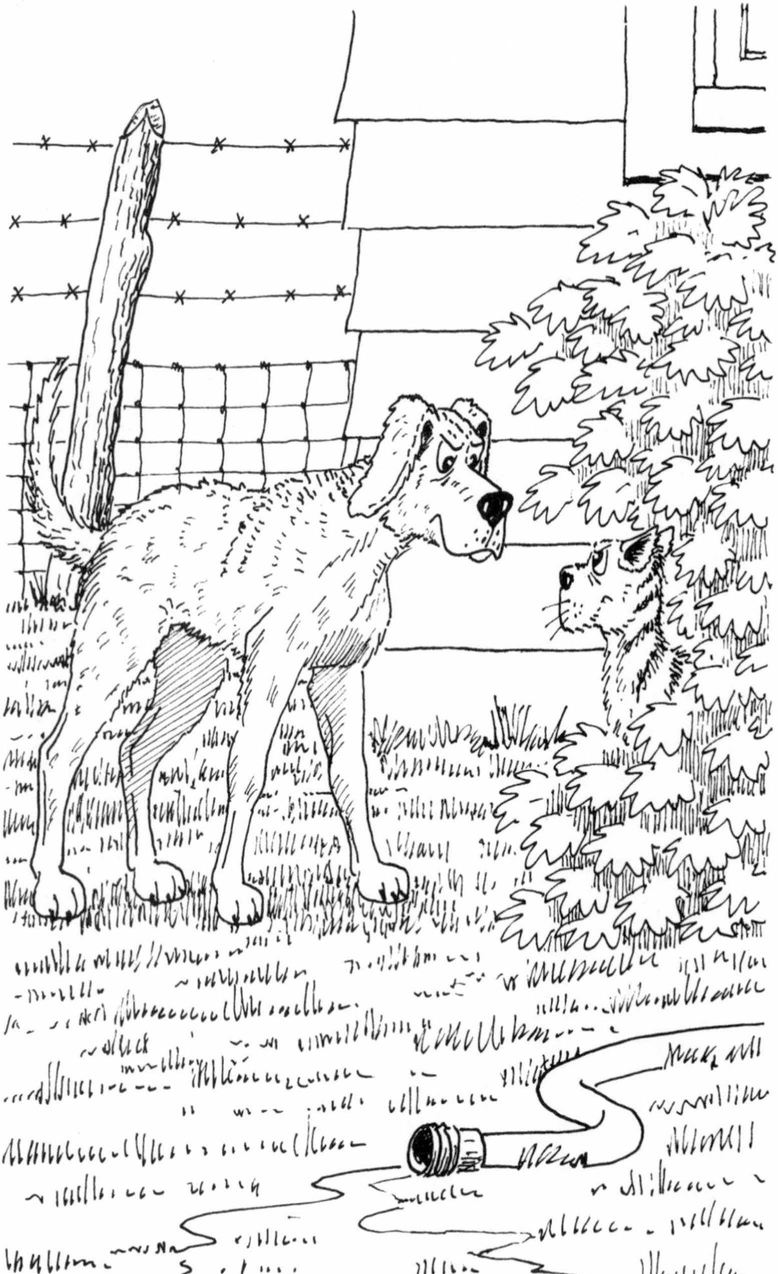

He studied me with hooded eyes. "I'd hate to guess, Hankie."

"Don't guess, Pete. It would be a waste of time. Let me tell you." I stuck my nose in his face, filled my chest with cold air, and gave him a blast of barking that, tee-hee, caused him to screech, hiss, hump his back, and go streaking out of the yard.

Tee-hee. I loved it. I LOVED IT! New meaning rushed into my life as I chased him up a tree. Yes sir, when dealing with cats, it's always best to go straight to the bottom line. As I marched back into the yard, holding my head at a triumphant angle, I realized that the little sneak had landed a few lucky punches to the end of my nose, but so what? Show me a dog without scabs on his nose and I'll show you a dog who hasn't done a proper job of humbling the kitties.

I had my scars and was proud of them. I marched back into the yard, with my head high so that all the world could see my scars and know that Hank the Cowdog does not take trash off the cats.

CHAPTER FIVE

I Discover a Pool of Spring Water

Drover saw my battle wounds, and as you might expect, he was deeply impressed. "Boy, Pete sure trashed your nose."

"Thanks, pal. Did you see what I did to him?"

"Well . . . maybe not."

"I gave him Full Air Horns in the face. I parted his hair, flattened his ears, rattled his teeth, blew his socks off."

"Yeah, but you're the only one wearing blood."

I towered over him and gave him a worldly smirk. "That's right, Drover, and I wear it proudly. Do you know what we call this?"

"Well, let's see. A bloody nose?"

"No."

"Uh . . . lacerations and hemorrhaging?"

44

"No."

"Well, let me think. Uh . . . facial trauma?"

I glared down into the emptiness of his eyes. "You've missed the whole point, Drover, and please stop showing off and using big words. Nobody is fooled by your childish expeditionism."

"You mean 'exhibitionism'?"

"I meant exactly what I said."

"What did you say?"

"I don't know what I said, but I said it and I meant every word of it."

"It was a big word."

"Of course it was a big word. Do you think I'd waste my time with scrawny little words? No sir. We should all strive to enlarge our respective vocabularies, Drover, and it wouldn't hurt you to use a big word every now and then."

He rolled his eyes. "Boy, I sure get confused. I thought you just told me . . ."

"Never mind. Let's return to my original question." I pointed to the scars on my nose. "What is another name for this?"

"Well . . . wreckage?"

"We're out of time and you've failed the quiz. I'm sorry."

"You couldn't help it."

"Thanks. It's called the Red Batch of Courage,

because it takes a batch of courage for a dog to accumulate all these scars. One of these days, maybe you'll win some."

"Not if I can help it."

"What? Speak up, you're muttering."

"I said . . . oh boy. Scars. Blood. Scabs. Just what I always wanted on my nose."

I gave him a little pat on the back. "It'll come, just be patient. And always remember, Drover: It's not the size of the fight in the kite that matters; it's the size of the fog in the dog."

He stared at me.

"Hello? Did you hear what I said?"

"Yeah, but I don't get it."

"That's as clear as I can make it, son. When you grow up, many of life's mysteries will be revealed. Until then, just watch me and study your lessons."

At that very moment, my lecture was brought to an end by Little Alfred, who had gone to the back door and was holding it open for us. "Come on, doggies, wet's go inside the house."

I went bounding across the yard and joined up with our little pal. But then I noticed that Drover was hanging back. "Hey, come on. What's the problem?"

"Well, we're not allowed in the house. Sally May . . ."

"Sally May's gone and she's left her son in command."

"That's scary."

"And besides, Slim is sick and needs us to nurse him back to health."

"Yeah, but what if Sally May comes home and finds us? She might cut off our tails with a butcher knife."

I heaved a sigh. "Drover, please. You already have a stub tail, so you've got nothing to lose."

"Yeah, but . . . what if she cuts off our heads?"

"Then your two ends will match. You'll have a stub head to go with your stub tail. Now come on and quit whining."

At last he joined us—not joyfully, I must say, but casting glances over his shoulders and looking as guilty as the cad who ate the canary . . . or whatever it is. He didn't look happy about entering the house, is the point.

I knew what to do when we got inside. I went straight to an old rug on the floor of Sally May's utility room—went straight to it and flopped down. Do you see the importance of this gesture? Maybe not. Let me explain.

See, when we dogs are invited into the house—which is very rarely—we feel honored to be there, and the way we express our feelings and so forth is to establish ourselves in the utility room, which is also known as the "mud room," the "laundry room," and the "take-off-the-dirty-boots room." It's the one room in the house, don't you see, that isn't as clean as all the other rooms in the house, which means that it's sort of a halfway chamber between the dirty outdoors and the clean inside.

When we dogs show a willingness to set up shop in the utility room, it sort of shows our great respect for the, uh, rest of the house. It says to our human friends, "Hey, we know we're just dirty dogs and we don't deserve to lie on the nice carpets or sleep in the chairs or do any of that other stuff that a dog might, uh, find pretty appealing."

It says, "Hey, this is great, no dog could ask for more, we're perfectly happy to be out here with the . . . well, dirty boots and soiled laundry and the cold draft that always seems to be coming under the back door."

You get it now? It impresses our human friends when they see a dog who's happy with simple gifts. Nobody likes a dog who has no class or manners, who goes loping through the house the minute he gets inside, as though he owns the place.

These little things are important.

The other side of the deal is that, once we've established ourselves as Happy Dogs in the Utility

Room, we can always . . . how can I say this? I wouldn't want to give the wrong impression. See, all of Life's Situations consist of a Plan A and a Plan B. The Happy Dogs Skinario is your basic Plan A, and once we've taken care of Plan A, we can go to work on, heh heh, Plan B.

At this point, I can't reveal the exact nature of Plan B. I mean, I wouldn't want anyone to think . . . you'll just have to figure it out for yourself. And I'll bet you'll never guess the true nature of our Plan B.

Okay. We were inside the house, out of the cold wind and swirling dust and so forth, and we were the happiest two dogs in the whole entire world. We couldn't have asked for more. We couldn't have dreamed or hoped for better. Being in a warm clean house was the fulfilament of our fondish wisses . . . fondest wishes, I should say, and even if Little Alfred had invited us to go deeper into the house—nay, even if he had *begged* us to venture into the warmer, more comfortable rooms of the house—it would have been our duty to turn him down.

"No thanks, kid. We're dogs. We know our place. We know your ma and understand her feelings about dogs in the house. No, the utility room is good enough for us."

49

So there we were, as happy as two clams in . . . something. A pot of clam chowder, I suppose, although if I were a clam . . .

So there we were, as happy as two dogs could be, and I want the record to show that we remained in this State of Utmost Contentment for . . . oh, five minutes or so. Ten minutes. A long long time. It seemed hours, actually, because . . . well, it was kind of boring out there, and also the floor was cold.

And I want the record to show that it was Drover who made the first move. All at once he raised his head. "Hank, I'm thirsty."

I raised my head and gave him a scowl. "How could you be thirsty? We're almost in winter, it's cold outside."

"I know, but I'm thirsty. I'm dying for a drink."

"Why didn't you get a drink outside? We have two stock tanks down at the corrals and two miles of Wolf Creek. That's where dogs are supposed to drink."

"Yeah, but I didn't know I was thirsty back then. And it was too far to walk."

"Oh brother."

"You're not thirsty?"

"No. Well, maybe a little, but I have something called Iron Discipline. I can wait."

"Boy, not me. I've got a terrible thirst, but where would a dog get a drink in here?"

"I don't know, Drover, nor do I care. Please stop complaining and try to show...hmm, I wouldn't mind a little drink myself, come to think of it."

I pushed myself up on all-fours and crept to the door that led into the kitchen and the rest of the house. Alfred was nowhere in sight, but I could hear voices coming from the living room. I lifted one ear and monitored the conversation.

Alfred: "How do you feel now, Swim?"

Slim: "I feel like warmed-over chicken manure. I ain't got any energy and all I want to do is sleep."

Alfred: "I bet you've got the measles."

Slim: "I ain't got the measles."

Alfred: "What about all those wed spots?"

Slim: "It's allergies. It's got nothing to do with measles. Let me sleep another hour. I'll be okay. Stay in the house and don't do anything foolish. And keep them dogs outside."

Alfred: "Okay, Swim."

As I was monitoring this conversation, I began to notice that...hmmm, my mouth was very dry, and all of a sudden I was dying for a drink of water. It's odd, how a sudden thirst will come upon a dog in the middle of winter, a time when you

51

wouldn't expect us to get thirsty. I suppose it comes from our busy schedules. I mean, in the wintertime a guy forgets to drink water, and then all at once . . .

I left the kitchen door and moved a few steps to the east. Here was another door which led into a small dark room. I peered into the gloom. All at once my nose, which is a very sensitive smellatory device, began picking up faint traces of . . . water.

Hey, we were making some progress. Drover had thought you couldn't find water inside the house. Ha. What did he know? I had found water because I'd had enough ambition to get up off my duff and go looking. Drover, on the other hand, had been content to stay on the rug and whine about it.

I tiptoed into the darkened room, following my nose toward the unmistable scent of fresh water. After going ten or twelve steps, I found the source. It was . . . it appeared to be a spring, a natural spring of fresh sparkling water—right there in the house!

Boy, what a nice surprise, and an even bigger surprise was that this spring came bubbling out of the ground into a big white bowl. I mean, it was the perfect height for dogs to drink out of. In fact, I began to suspect that it had been put there for this very purpose. Can you believe that? Sally May had developed this nice little spring, just so her son's loyal dogs could get a drink when they came into the house.

She was a pretty fine old gal, that Sally May.

Anyways, I hopped up on my back legs, stuck my head into the bowl, and started lapping. Lap, lap, lap. Great water, and yes, I'd been pretty thirsty, even though . . .

HUH?

All of a sudden . . . well, you'll see.

CHAPTER SIX

We Fix Slim a
Nourishing Lunch

Someone or something had turned on the light.
All at once I found myself staring into . . .
well, into this big white porcelain urn, out which
I had been drinking, and then I heard a voice
behind me that said, "Hankie! Get out of the
bathroom. Don't dwink out of the pot!"

Huh? Okay, it appeared that I had . . . it
wasn't exactly a spring, see, but in the gloomi-
ness of the darkness I had . . .

Well, where's a dog supposed to drink in the
house? If they don't put out pans of water, what's
a poor thirsty dog supposed to do, get a pitcher of
orange juice out of the ice box? I mean, water's
water, whether it comes out of the ground or out
of the pot, and I didn't see anything wrong . . .

Nevertheless, I felt embarrassed on being caught and exposed, and I darted past Little Alfred and returned to my rug on the utility room floor. I sure didn't want him to think . . .

Drover met me with his usual silly grin. "Did you get in trouble for drinking out of the pot?"

"Yes, I did, and I hope you're happy, since you're the one who started the whole thing."

"I was?"

"Yes, by moaning and complaining about how thirsty you were. I wasn't thirsty at all until you started moaning about it. Now look what you've caused."

"Yeah, I feel terrible about it."

"Good. I hope the guilt eats your liverwurst."

"But you know what? I'm not thirsty anymore. After what you said about self-discipline, I decided I could wait. I guess you were right, 'cause it worked. Are you proud of me?"

I studied him with narrowed eyes. "Drover, sometimes I think you're trying to make a mockery of my position as Head of Ranch Security, and I'm afraid this will have to go into my report."

"Gosh, did I do something wrong?"

"No. You did something right, and it has thrown everything out of balance. You need to work on consistency. How can I run this ranch . . . just skip it."

We curled up in our respective spots on the rug and settled back into the business of being Good Dogs in the House. The minutes crawled by. Drover fell right off to sleep and began his usual concert of weird sounds—grunting, squeaking, and wheezing. I couldn't sleep. Who could sleep with such noise?

I lifted my head and happened to glance out the window. Good grief, it was SNOWING, and we're talking about big flakes and a lot of 'em. I crept over to the window and looked out. Yes, by George, it was snowing hard, and that wind was already whipping it up into drifts.

The lights blinked. Uh-oh, that was a bad almond. Omen. Whatever. If that old wind kept blowing the electric lines around, it could knock out the power to all the houses along the creek. No power, no lights. No power, no heater for the house. I wondered if Slim knew . . . no, of course he didn't. He was sick and asleep in the other room.

It occurred to me that I had better go check this out. I mean, with Loper and Sally May gone to Abilene, and with Slim sick in bed . . . gee, that left me and Little Alfred in charge of things. In my deepest heart, I knew that Sally May would want me to leave the, uh, utility room and venture into other parts of the house to, well, give aid and comfort to her little boy.

And so it was that I crept to the door that led into the kitchen and peeked inside. There was Little Alfred, standing on a chair and doing something on the counter beside the sink. I crept forward, one step at a time, on paws that were trained to make no sound at all, until I reached the middle of the kitchen. There, I sat down and assumed a pose that we call "I've Been Here All Along and You Just Didn't Notice Me."

It must have worked. He saw me out of the corner of his eye and said, "I'm making Swim some cowboy hash. He's too sick to get up."

Sure enough, he had opened a can of . . . something . . . hash, it appeared, and was spooning it into a cooking pot. What a nice idea, and what a clever lad. These ranch kids will surprise you. In hard times, when they're called upon to . . . it smelled pretty yummy, that hash, and I found myself sniffing the air and more or less inching my way closer to his, uh, location.

Anyways, these ranch kids are pretty resourceful and that hash was smelling better by the second, and I continued to inch my way in Alfred's direction. By this time my ears were perked and I was licking my chops and wondering about the possibility of . . . well, testing the hash, so to speak. I mean, your better cooks and chefs do that. They call in impartial judges to try out a certain dish or recipe, just to make sure . . .

I laid my head and nose upon the seat of the chair, right beside his feet, and gave my eyes an upward roll. Oh, and I also went to Helpful Taps on the tail section, just to call his attention to the fact that . . . well, I was there and ready to lend a hand in the task of, uh, feeding the sick and wounded.

He must have heard the tapping. He grinned down at me and said, "You want a bite?"

Well, I . . . I certainly didn't want to intrude into

his . . . I mean, I realized that he was very busy,
but one little bite . . . or what the heck, one big bite
might be, uh, very nice.

Yes.

He put the spoon in front of my nose. My eyes
sprang open and my ears leaped upward, but
you'll be proud to know that I resisted the temp-
tation to *gobble* the hash. That's what your ordinary run of ranch mutts would have done—
gobbled and slobbered and wolfed it down. Not
me, fellers. This was Sally May's house and her

good influence was still present in the atmosphere, guiding and directing me toward a more refined and mannerly approach to, uh, the eating of hash from a spoon.

I ate it in the most dainty fashion you can imagine, using my front teeth, tongue, and lips. This was no gobbling deal, and I think even Little Alfred was impressed. I did spill one piece of hash . . . two small pieces . . . okay, several fragments of hash fell to the floor, but I had 'em cleaned up in no time at all. Sally May would never know.

And yes, that was some pretty awesome hash, great stuff and . . . could we try that again, just one more time?

I filled the space between Alfred and me with Looks of Longing. I laid my chin upon his foot and tapped my tail on the floor. He laughed and said, "No more, Hankie. I'm making this for Swim."

Well, yes, sure, I knew that, but . . . and I would have been the first to admit that Slim deserved the biggest portion of it, I mean, him sick and everything, but still . . .

No sale.

He picked up a bottle of ketchup and hammered on the bottom of it until a big blob of it . . . oops, he missed the pan and the ketchup went on the floor, but that was no problem. Hey,

I was there to help, and cleaning up little ketchup spills was no big deal to me.

I shined the floor with my tongue. Ketchup wasn't exactly my favorite food. It's made out of tomaters, don't you know, and a lot of your ranch dogs wouldn't touch the stuff, because it doesn't have any meat in it, but I licked it up, every drop of it, because . . . well, because of my deep feelings of loyalty to Sally May. We sure didn't want her coming home to a house that was all splattered with ketchup splots.

Alfred gripped the spoon in his fist and stirred the ketchup into the hash. Then he tasted it. "Mmmmm. Swim's gonna wike this."

He climbed down from the chair, scooted it across the floor to the stove, climbed up on the chair again, and turned on the front burner. Whilst he was doing all this, he . . . uh . . . set the pot of hash down on the floor, don't you see, and he wasn't watching and I saw no great harm in . . . Heh, heh. He didn't notice.

He picked up the pot, climbed up on the chair, and set the pot on the burner. Good idea. A little shot of heat would help the taste. It was exactly the sort of thing Slim never would have done, he being a bit of a lazy chef, but warm hash was always better than cold hash.

Whilst the hash was warming on the stove, Alfred scooted the chair over to one of the cabinets above the sink. He opened the cabinet door and reached on tiptoes for a plate. Gee, this WAS a fancy deal. Slim was going to eat his hash on a real plate! That was another thing he wouldn't have done. He would have eaten right out of the pot, because washing plates was too much . . .

CRASH!

Uh-oh. In the process of pulling a plate out of the cabinet, the boy must have bumped a jar of . . . what was that stuff? The jar hit the countertop, see, and the lid flew off and now something thick and yellowish was spreading across the counter and oozing down the cabinets.

I moved toward it and sniffed. My goodness, it seemed that we had us a little spill of honey, and it was a derned good thing I happened to be there. I went right to work on it and . . .

Smoke? Where was all that smoke coming from? Oh, the hash. Alfred had left the burner on high, it appeared, and the hash had begun to hiss and pop. I barked the alarm, and Alfred pushed his chair . . . oops, right through some of the honey . . . pushed his chair back over to the stove and got the fire shut down.

Through the smoke, I saw his grin. "I hope

Swim wikes barbecued hash." He stepped down . . . oops, right in some more of the honey and pushed the chair back over to the . . . I guess he wasn't paying attention to the honey mess, and he sure was making it worse.

Anyways, he finally succeeded in spooning the barbecued hash onto the plate, and at that point he beamed me a big smile. "There. Swim's gonna be pwoud of this." Carrying the plate in front of him like a chef, he marched through the house and presented it to our fallen comrade.

I don't suppose he noticed the honey footprints, but I did, and I went right to work scrubbing Sally May's floor. I cleaned up most of the mess on the limoleun . . . limoneum . . . lino . . . whatever . . . on the floor in the kitchen, but I didn't know what to do about the tracks on the carpet. Maybe no one would notice.

That's the great thing about carpet. You never have to clean it. Mud, dirt, honey, dog hair. It never shows. Great stuff, that carpet.

Anyways, I guess Slim was pretty hungry and was glad to get the grub, even though it was a little scorched in spots. I heard the spoon clanking on the plate and heard Slim say that it was the best hash he'd ever eaten.

But just then, several things happened. First,

the electricity went out and the house fell into semidarkness. Second, the phone rang. Back in the depths of the house, I heard Slim grumble, "No, I'll get it. I ain't *that* sick."

A moment later he dragged himself into the kitchen and snatched the phone off the wall. He looked . . . pretty bad. His face was splotched with red, his eyes were puffy and had a pinched look, his hair stuck up in the back and fell over his brow in the front. He looked weak and tired and . . . well, sick.

"Hello. Yes. No, she ain't here. They went to Abilene. Yalp. Uh-huh. Who is this? Viola? I'll be derned. I never would have expected . . . hold on a minute, Viola."

I was busy scrubbing floors, but when his voice trailed off, I lifted my head. I noticed that his eyes were locked on . . . something. Something on the kitchen counter, near the sink. The empty hash can?

He blinked his eyes and turned to Alfred. "Button, is that the can you got my hash out of?" Alfred nodded. "Hey Viola, I just ate a plate of *dog food*."

D og food?

I took a closer look at the can. So did Little Alfred. Until this very moment, neither of us had noticed the picture of a German shepherd on the label, but there he was. Well, it sure fooled me, and it sure fooled Slim too. Don't forget, he's the one who'd said it was the best hash he'd ever eaten.

Well, this was a strange turn of events. Neither I nor Alfred knew quite how to respond to it. Under different circumstances, we might have gotten a big laugh out of it, I mean, you must admit that it was pretty funny. But with Slim sick to start with and talking on the phone to his lady friend . . . well, it just didn't seem the proper time to go into fits and gales of laughter.

Slim wasn't laughing. After giving me and Alfred some hot glares, he returned to his phone conversation.

"Hello? Viola, you still there? Yes, I'm serious. Button opened up a can and thought it was hash, only it was dog food. Uh-huh, every bite. Well, I thought it was pretty good, until I seen the can. Yes, I feel a little sick, but I felt sick before I ate it. Oh, just a little cold, is all. Button thinks it's the measles but I'm sure it ain't. Grown men don't get . . ."

He scowled. "They *do*? Pretty bad, huh? Well, that part fits. I'd have to feel better to die. Red spots? No, I don't have any."

Alfred was listening to Slim's end of the conversation, and his face showed astonishment. "Swim, you do too have wed spots!"

"Shhh. Just hush. We don't want to get her all stirred up. Huh? Oh, I was just talking to my chef. After feeding me dog food hash, now he's trying to play doctor. He thinks I've got red spots but I'm pretty sure . . . Mirror? Well, yes, I reckon there's . . . I'll be derned, I'm standing right in front of one."

He squinted into the mirror. His eyebrows jumped. "Viola, you still there? What would it mean if a guy's whole face was splotched with

66

red? Huh. I'll be derned. Well . . . supposing a feller had measles, what would he do for 'em?" He gave a wooden laugh. "Well, we can skip over that part, I ain't going to the doctor. Me and doctors don't . . . no."

He held the phone away from his ear for a few seconds, then went back to it. "You still there? No, it ain't that I'm stubborn and mule-headed. It's just . . . okay, I'm stubborn and mule-headed, and I ain't going to the doctor." His gaze went to the window. "Good honk, did you know it's snowing outside? Well, there's my reason right there. I ain't going to town in a snowstorm. Huh? Well, if it quits snowing, I still ain't . . ."

His expression darkened. "No, I wouldn't hear of it. No, I ain't sick, I'm feeling better already. Honest. Them red spots are just about gone. Viola? Hello?" He hung up the phone and gave us a scowl. "Arguing with her is like arguing with petrified wood. I reckon she's going to try to drive up here in her daddy's pickup, and I ain't got the energy to fight her. And you know what else? When she gets that thing stuck in a snowdrift, I ain't going to have the energy to go pull her out. I'm going to bed—in the bedroom."

Dragging his feet across the floor, he started toward the bedroom. All at once he stopped, picked up one foot, and felt it. "What's that sticky stuff on the floor?" Silence fell over the room, as Alfred and I studied the, uh, patterns and so forth on the, uh, wallpaper. "Never mind. I don't want to know, but you knotheads just remember: if Sally May comes home and decides to kill me, y'all will be next on her list."

With that, he dragged himself through the darkened house. We could hear him muttering to himself. "I don't know how I get in these messes. And Viola's out running around in a snowstorm. Stubborn woman."

We heard the bed squeak as he collapsed into it. Alfred and I exchanged worried glances. Then he jerked his head toward the bedroom and we went creeping through the . . . yes, that floor was pretty sticky, all right, and I sure hoped we'd have time to clean it up.

We crept into the bedroom. There was Slim, stretched out, with the covers pulled up to his chin. His eyes were shut. Alfred's gaze went from Slim to me, then back to Slim.

"Hey Swim, are you asweep?"

His eyes drifted open. "Not yet, just driftin' that way."

"I'm sorry I fixed you a pwate of dog food. I didn't mean to, honest."

A faint smile dashed across Slim's mouth and he waved his hand through the air. "I know you didn't, Button. Don't worry about it. What's good for a ranch dog can't be too bad for a cowboy, I reckon. And to tell you the truth, it tasted better than what I'm used to."

The boy's lip began to tremble. "Swim, I don't want you to be sick, and I'm scared."

"Well, don't be scared. Maybe Viola'll make it. You watch the clock, Button. If she ain't here in an hour, you come wake me up, hear? Maybe I can . . ."

His eyes closed and he drifted off to sleep. The boy bit his lip and we went back into the kitchen. He cast a worried glance at the big flakes of snow that were swirling at the west window, then turned to me.

"Hankie, I can't tell time on a cwock. Can you?"

Me? Heck no, I was just a dog.

He thought about it for a minute, then his eyes lit up. "I know. My mom's got a timer. She uses it for cooking, and when you turn the dial all the way awound, it means one hour."

He ran for his all-purpose ladder (the chair) and scooted it over to the sink. He climbed up onto the counter and . . . hey, watch out for the . . . SPLOSH . . . he stepped right into a pool of

69

honey on the counter, opened up the cabinet door, and plucked the timer from the highest shelf. He held it up and gave me a smile.

Great, but I wondered what he would do about that . . . he didn't do anything, except pull his foot out of it and climb back down to the floor. I found myself staring the, uh, sticky honey track on the floor. I tapped my tail several times, hoping he might get the message about the mess, but he didn't. It went right over his head. I guess he was so excited about solving the timer problem that he didn't notice anything else.

He twisted the thing as far as it would go to the left . . . right . . . he twisted the thing as far as it would go and it started ticking. He set it on the kitchen table, and to reach the table he had to walk across . . .

More honey tracks. *She was going to kill us.* She was going to come home from Abilene, march us out into a snowbank, and shoot us all. I'm no fuss-budget about cleanliness, but even I could see that we were wrecking her house beyond all repair. And when I say WE, I mean HIM. He was going to get us all shot by his very own mother.

I mean, a dog can lick up a few spots here and there, but our tongues were never intended to be mops, for crying out loud. Have you ever tried to

mop a whole house with your tongue? It's impossible, it's . . .

Oh well. There was nothing I could do about it. I would try to enjoy my last days upon this earth. I'd had a pretty good life. I'd always thought it might be a little longer, but . . . boy, the thought of seeing Sally May when she walked into that house gave me the shivers.

We could run away from home. Yes, Alfred and I would pack a lunch and flee into the blizzard, become savages and live off the land. He could dress himself in . . . something. Leaves or rabbit skins. We'd find a cave and make it our home. After a couple of years, maybe Sally May would simmer down and take us back.

On the other hand, that old wind was sure howling out there, and the more I thought about running off into a blizzard, the less excited I felt about trying it.

Well, once Alfred had set the timer, we had nothing to do but . . . wait. You know about me and waiting. I hate it. Once a guy has developed an active mind, it's hard for him to adjust to the slow rhythms of . . . and you know what made it worse? The ticking of the derned timer. It made time pass even slower than it would have otherwise.

Ho hum.

Well, I figured I might as well start mopping the floor. It had to be done, and I had good reason for thinking that Alfred wouldn't get around to doing it. He was an expert on making messes, but not so good at cleaning them up.

I started licking honey tracks. It was kind of pleasant work, actually. I mean, if a guy's going to lick the floor, honey tracks are a pretty good thing to lick. The problem was that *they were all over the place.* How could . . . oh well . . . the job seemed overwhelming.

I had been mopping for, oh, ten or fifteen minutes when Alfred broke the silence. "Hankie, the house is getting code."

I mopped stopping, I mean stopped mopping,

and glanced around. He was right. The power hadn't come back on and the house was losing heat. I gave him a look that said, "Right. So . . . what can we do about that?"

"If the ewectwicity stays off, the pwumbing might fweeze."

Yikes, I hadn't thought of that. Have we discussed Frozen Plumbing? Maybe not, but it's about the worst thing that can happen in the winter. I had been through this a time or two down at Slim's place, so I guess we could say that I was . . . well, something of an expert on Ranch Plumbing.

See, when your heater goes off, the temperature inside the house begins to drop. If it drops far enough, the water pipes freeze. Do you know what happens to water pipes when they freeze? They bust. Burst. Break. Whatever. Even pipes made of steel will break, and then when they thaw out, guess what they do.

They leak. They spurt water in bad places, such as under the house, under the sink, in the attic, and boy, you talk about an unholy mess! Busted pipes could ruin a house.

Yes, we had a problem here, and to show my concern, I began sweeping my tail across . . . that is, my tail got hung in some of that honey on the floor and I found it impossible to do Slow Sweeps, so I was forced to rise to my feet and go to Slow Thoughtful Wags.

Yes, we had us a problem.

Alfred chewed his lip, whilst I attended to the Slow Wags.

"Do you weckon we ought to build a fire in the woodstove?"

By ourselves? Without Slim? Uh . . . no, bad idea. Better let Slim do it.

The boy thought for a moment. "We need the fire, Hankie. I'll go tell Swim."

Good thinking.

He went into the bedroom and I heard the murmur of their voices. When the boy returned, he said, "Swim said for me and you to bwing in the wood, then he'll get up and wight the fire."

And so it was that we launched ourselves into the task of loading up the woodstove.

CHAPTER EIGHT

The Red-Eyed Mummy Monster Appears

Oh, there was one other problem I forgot to mention: Little Alfred's furry slippers.

You might recall that he'd been walking through honey with them, and they were . . . well, you can imagine. Furry slippers + honey is a real bad combination. They were a mess, and every time he took a step, he spread the mess to other parts of the house.

It wasn't easy, but I managed to get the point across to him that he needed to park those dadgum slippers, and maybe even burn 'em in the stove. It took all my vast skills as a communicator to convince him of this—an unusually large number of wags and whimpers and nose-pointings, but at last he figured out that honeyed slippers leave tracks.

Whew. That was a toughie.

He changed into his boots, pulled on his coat, and we went out the back door to bring in some firewood. Oh, and when Alfred opened that back door, a gust of cold wind greeted us and I had to listen to Drover whimper and cry. He was curled up in a little white ball on the rug, and shivering. Do you suppose he offered to help, lend a hand, join the cause? Oh no. He moaned and complained and said he was freezing to death.

The little weenie. Sometimes I think . . . oh well. That was typical Drover—helpless in a crisis and worthless to the end.

We went outside, Alfred and I, and fellers, it didn't take us long to figure out that this was a vicious storm. That wind was so strong and cold, it took our breath away, and we could hardly see through the swirling snow.

It was hard to believe that the day had begun warm and clear, that only hours ago, we had enjoyed a calm fall day. But that's the way it is with storms on the prairie. They come out of nowhere, without warning, and strike with

the fury of a demon. That's how people in the old days froze to death. I guess.

What do I know about the old days? Forget it.

We staggered through the drifts that were beginning to pile up in the yard, stumbled through the swirls of snow.

And yes, it was a little scary. I mean, I'm not the kind of dog who often feels small and insignificant, but the raw brutal power of that storm made me feel...well, small and insignificant. Alfred noticed it too. I felt his hand searching for me, and he held me close as we made our way to the woodpile.

He made a cradle of his arms (he'd seen his dad do it many times) and loaded it with several sticks of . . . whatever kind of wood it was. Hackberry, chinaberry, cedar, cottonwood. Slim and Loper cut up all the dead trees on the ranch, see, and used it for stovewood, so a guy was never sure what kind of wood he might be throwing into the stove.

As you might have guessed, I wasn't able to carry much wood, just one small branch of kindling in my mouth. The boy had to do most of the heavy work on this deal, but I led the way back to the house. We dropped our wood on the utility room floor and went back for another load.

And yes, Drover sat up long enough to complain about all the cold air we were letting into the house.

Back and forth we went, until we had a fair-sized pile of wood inside the house. By that time, we were both plastered with snow and exhausted from the effort.

When Alfred had closed the door for the last time, he heaved a sigh and shook his head. "Miss Viowa's never gonna make it. It's awful." The ends of his mouth turned down. "Hankie, I'm scared. I wish my mommy and daddy were here."

His cheeks were red from the cold, and I had to lick some of the snow off his face. Yes, it was a scary time, and all of us wished his folks were there. But they weren't, and we had to buck up and be brave and do our jobs.

We needed to get that fire going in the stove.

Alfred carried several sticks of wood through the house and into the living room, where the big cast-iron stove was located. I tried not to notice all the tracks we left on the floor, but we left plenty of them—mud and melted snow. I made a mental note to go back later and clean up the mess.

As we passed through the kitchen, we paused to look at the timer. Forty-five minutes had passed. Miss Viola hadn't made it yet.

Alfred opened up the door of the stove and looked inside. "How does my dad start the fire?"

We studied the situation together. I wasn't sure. I mean, I had been in the room when Slim had fired up his stove, and I knew there were some tricks to building a fire in a cold stove. But what were the tricks?

Wait. Something about . . . the draft.

Yes, that was it, the draft. You had to get a hot fire going so that the smoke and so forth would go up the chimney. A cold chimney didn't draw air as well as a hot one, so we needed . . . newspapers. That's what they started with, wadded up newspapers, and once they got the newspapers to burning, they added small sticks of kindling.

Newspapers, kindling, then logs. Alfred made a little teepee of kindling around the paper. Now all we needed was Slim to approve our work and do the final honors of striking the match. Alfred went for him. It took a while to wake him up, but at last he appeared at the door—red-eyed, scowling, hair down in his eyes.

He looked . . . pretty bad.

He came over to the stove and studied our work. "Huh. Not bad for an orphan child and a souphound. She ought to light, if that wood ain't too wet."

He struck the match and lit the newspaper. A little yellow flame began nibbling at the papers. We held our breath. It grew and grew . . . but then a big gust of wind came down the chimney and blew it out. Smoke came back into our faces and into the room.

Slim tried it again, and this time the smoke began curling up the chimney. He added more paper and kindling. The wood hissed and sizzled. Everything was wet from the snow. It wasn't going to burn. But then, with a little pop, the kindling caught fire and began to glow and grow.

Slim looked down at us with his soggy eyes. "I'm going back to bed. Come get me in five minutes and I'll add some bigger chunks. You done good, boy." He went back to bed. We were a couple of heroes, no question about it.

We were sitting there, watching the fire and feeling proud of ourselves, when a heavy gust of wind rattled the house. It came down the chimney and started filling the room with smoke. And fellers, we're not talking about a little puff of smoke, the kind we'd had before. This was a whole CLOUD of smoke that filled the living room and moved into the rest of the house.

We both coughed and gasped and ran into the kitchen. Guess who met us there. Drover.

"Oh my gosh, Hank, I think the house is on fire. Help, murder, mayday, fire, fire! Oh my leg, let me out!"

I watched him squeak and run in circles. "Drover, please try to control yourself. The house is not on fire."

"Then what's all this smoke doing in here? Where there's smoke, there's bound to be a fire. Help!"

"True up to a point, Drover. There is indeed smoke and there is indeed fire, but it happens that the fire..." I found myself coughing "... it happens that the fire... hark, hack, honk... it happens... arg, honk... skip it, Drover, I can't breathe."

"Yeah, 'cause the house is burning down."

"The house is not . . . hark, honk!"

"What'll I do? If I stay in here, I'll fry."

"Then go outside."

"I'll freeze."

"Stand on your head. Sit on a tack. I don't care what you do."

"See? I knew you didn't care."

"I care. What more can I say?"

"Well . . . you could say the house isn't really on fire."

I looked into the vacuum of his eyes. "I already told you that."

"Yeah, but I didn't believe you."

"If I said it again, would you believe me?"

"Well . . . I don't know. I guess we could try."

"Fine. Drover, the house is on fire and you're going to get fried like the weenie you really are."

His jaw dropped and he stared at me.

"Do you believe me or not?"

"I . . . think not."

"Great. We solved that one. Go back to bed."

He gave me a puzzled look, shrugged, and trotted back out to the utility room, curled up, and went back to sleep. You know, that is the weirdest little mutt I ever saw, heard, or dreamed of.

Well, disposing of Drover brought us some

peace and quiet. Unfortunately, the smoke cloud remained—and in fact, it had gotten thicker and worse. Alfred's eyes were watering and he grabbed a tea towel and covered his nose and mouth with it.

"Hankie, I think we did something wong wiff the stove, 'cause it nots 'posed to make all this smoke."

Right. Hark! Yes, we'd obviously missed a step somewhere. I couldn't imagine what it was but . . .

HUH?

The last thing I expected to see just then—and I mean the VERY last thing in the whole world I expected to see just then—was a . . . Red-Eyed Mummy Monster . . . a huge Red-Eyed Mummy Monster wrapped in a sheet. And I couldn't be a hundred percent certain that he planned to eat me and Little Alfred, but he certainly gave me that impression.

You think I'm kidding, don't you?

You think I was seeing things or exaggerating, don't you?

Ha! I wish.

This was not only the first Red-Eyed Mummy Monster I had ever seen, but it was the first one who had ever offered to eat me—bones, hair, toenails, eyeballs, the whole shebang.

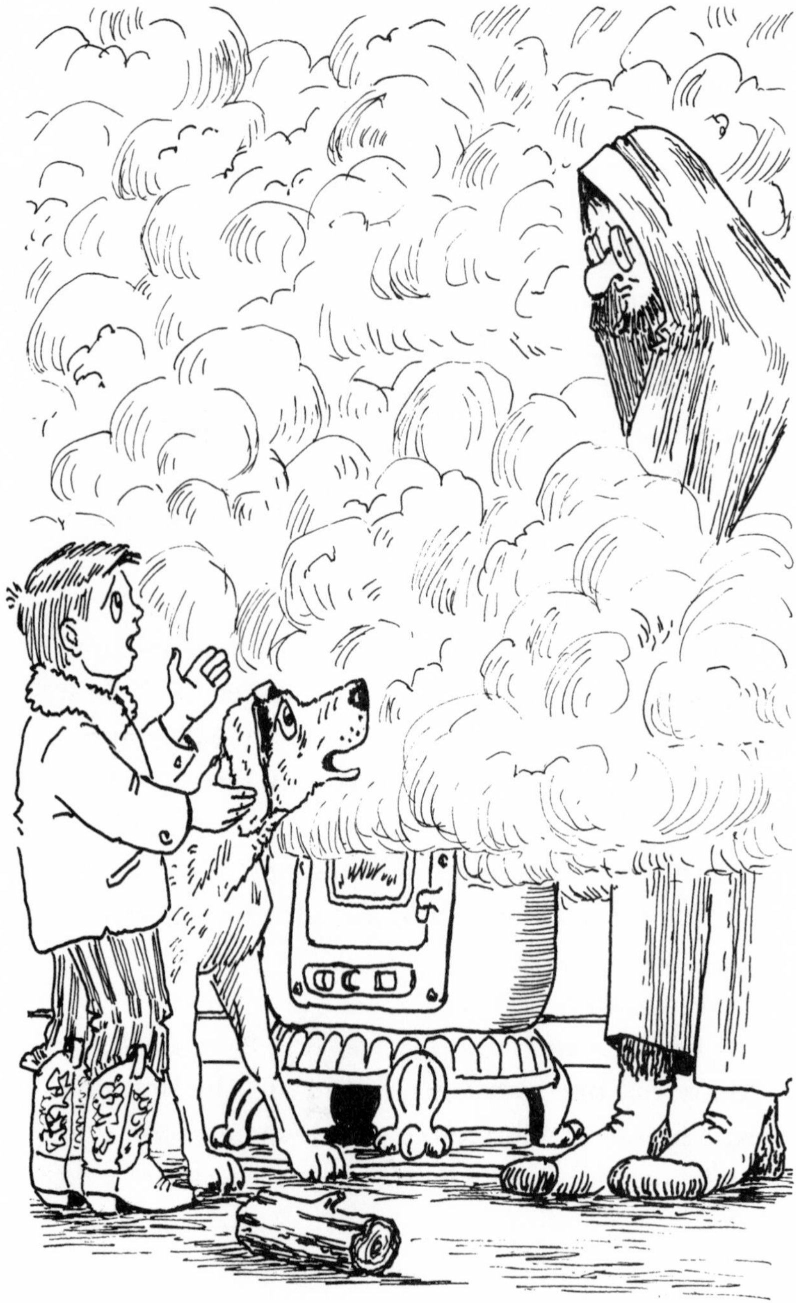

CHAPTER NINE

Alfred Shouldn't Have Tried to Drive the Pickup

He stared at me.
I stared at him.

The hair on my back shot up. His fell over his forehead and into his horrible red eyes.

A growl leaped into the deepest lurch of my throatalary region. He answered with a . . . I wasn't sure what it was. A growl. A grunt. A groan. It wasn't a bark, but it was enough to convince me that I needed to get out of there.

We're talking about Rapid Exit, fellers. I didn't know where I was going and I didn't know how I was going to put distance between me and that Mummy Monster when my feet were spinning on

the slick limoleun floor, but I was fairly determined to GET THE HECK OUT OF THERE!

Real determined.

I didn't know what Little Alfred planned to
do, but I made a dash for the cabinet under Sally
May's . . . BONK . . . sink, only the stupid door
was closed and, okay, I had no choice but to leap
up on the counter and then dive through the window, I mean, I was *that* scared and *that* determined to get away from that horrible awful
Mummy Monster.

So I went into a deep crouch and then exploded
upward, landed on the counter with all four . . .
honey? Okay, I landed in the honey puddle with
all four feet, but at least I was on my way out of
that scary place, and once on the counter . . .
once in the stupid honey puddle . . . I had tried to
warn Little . . .

But we had no time for that, no time to mourn
over what might have been or should have been,
fellers, I wanted out, OUT, O-U-T. So once I had
enscumbered myself upon the counter, I turned
and began the process of targeting my huge
enormous body toward the window and plotting
my . . .

YIPES!!

He was slouching in my direction, staring at

me with those ... those ... those horrible squinty puffy red eyes that were filled with ... I don't know what, but here he came, slouching and slumping in my direction like ... like ... like the corpse of a dead-bodied mummy, is what he looked like to me.

And without bothering to look where I was going, I slammed the old gear shift up into Road Gear and went flying ... into a canister of flour, and what a dumb place to put a canister of flour!

Who had been so careless as to put a canister of flour on the kitchen counter? This was an outrage, and I couldn't be held responsible for the, uh, flour mess that occurred when the, uh, canister flew off the counter and hit the ... well, the floor.

A huge omnivorous silence fell upon us, as all of us, even the Monster Mummy, stared at the . . . gee, what a mess, but I refused to be held . . .

He spoke. The Mummy Monster spoke. Here's what he said: "Did y'all happen to notice the house is full of smoke?"

The voice sounded . . . sort of . . . familiar. Okay, maybe . . . forget the business about the Mummy Monster. What we had here . . . it was just Slim, see, wrapped up in a sheet, but he sure looked . . .

He continued. "The house is full of smoke because some birdbrain forgot to open the damper." Alfred and I exchanged glances. "Under the circumstances, I'll have to give myself credit for that mess, but this . . ." He shot out a bony finger at the . . . uh . . . flour and so forth. "Somebody's neck is liable to get wrung over this deal, and it ain't going to be mine."

Just then we were saved by the bell. No kidding. Remember the timer Alfred had set down on the kitchen table? Well, just at that very exact moment, it went off, causing Slim to jump. He stared at it, then sank into a chair and dragged some of the hair out of his eyes.

"What's that for?" Alfred told him. He nodded. "I tried to tell her. Stubborn woman. And like I said, I ain't got the energy to go lookin' for her. He heaved a sigh. "Button, for future reference, you can't build a fire in the stove without the damper open."

"Okay, Swim."

He pushed himself up out of the chair. "I'll open the damper and chunk up the fire, and then I'm going back to bed. Y'all better start cleaning up that . . . boy, I can't stay awake."

On his way back to bed, he opened the damper and threw some logs into the stove. Opening the damper helped a bunch. All at once the smoke started going up the chimney instead of into the house.

We heard the bed springs groan and squeak under his weight. Moments later, the sounds of thirty-two head of wild hogs reached our ears. Okay, it was his snoring, but it sounded as loud as a bunch of wild hogs.

Anyways, he was gone again and Little Alfred and I were alone again. We looked at the flour mess on the floor—some of which, by the way, had combined with the previous honey mess. We both fell into deepest despair.

"Hankie, what if Viowa's stuck in a snowdwift?"

Well, if she was stuck in a snowdrift, she was . . . stuck in a snowdrift. What else could you say? Nobody on our place could help her.

Alfred was thinking about something. I could see at a glance that whatever he was thinking about didn't involve cleaning up his mother's kitchen. That worried me. At last he revealed his thoughts.

"Hankie, I bet we could dwive the pickup and go find Viowa."

I stared at him. He wasn't kidding. Him, drive the pickup out into . . . that was the craziest idea I'd heard in . . . no, I wanted no part of such . . . go out in this howling storm? NO!

"I think we could do it. I know how to dwive the pickup."

Oh yeah, sure. When Slim was there to start it up and put it in gear. That wasn't driving, that was *steering*. I turned my back on him and assumed the Pose of Shunning.

I heard his steps behind me. He seemed to be heading . . .

"Well, I'm going to twy. You and Dwover can come if you want, or y'all can stay here and be chickens."

Chickens! Since when was it chicken to use sound judgment, to be mature, to be . . . okay, okay, if the little snipe was going out into the storm, I needed to be there to protect him from . . . this was crazy.

We marched out into the utility room. Alfred found a pair of warm gloves and a wool stocking cap. Whilst he was pulling them on, I turned to the ball of white fur on the floor.

"Get up, Drover. We're going out on a rescue mission."

His head came up and his eyes crossed. "Out in this storm?"

"That's correct. If it weren't snowing, we wouldn't need a rescue mission. All these things fit together."

"Yeah, but . . . what about my leg?"

"Bring it along. This is All Hands on Deck."

"Yeah, but I don't have any hands. All I've got is feet."

"That's close enough. Move out, soldier, and I don't want to hear any more of your opinions."

He whined and moaned, but I ignored him. Alfred opened the door and we trooped out into the . . . gag, that wind was terrible! It took our breath away. We could hardly see the yard gate through the blowing snow.

Drover moaned and shivered. "I want to go home!"

"Hush. You are home. Home is where the heart is."

"My heart's frozen!"

"Look at the bright side, Drover. As long as your heart is frozen, you'll never get heartburn."

"This is crazy and that's not funny."

"I'm sorry, son, it's the best I can do. Now hush."

We lowered our heads into the wind and followed the boy across the snowdrifted yard, out the gate, and up the hill to the place where Slim had parked the pickup. If we were lucky, Alfred wouldn't be able to start it. Then we could go back into the house, satisfied that we had done our best.

We reached the pickup. The windblown snow hit our faces like BBs. Alfred reached up, seized the door handle, and pulled the door open, struggling against the wind. When he finally got it open, he pointed inside.

Okay, here went nothing. I nudged Mister Squeakbox with my nose. He jumped inside and I followed. We sat down on the . . . that was the coldest pickup seat I had ever experienced! It was hard, brittle, and frigid, and my hiney wasn't proud of me for making it sit down on such a block of ice.

Alfred struggled his way into the cab and the wind slammed the door behind him. The wind was rocking the pickup. Our respective breaths made balloons of fog in the air.

Okay, now what?

Alfred sat down behind the wheel. Good grief, he couldn't even see over the dashboard! How was he going to ... this would never work. We could only hope that he wouldn't remember how to start the engine.

But he was thinking about it. I could see that. He was trying to remember all the steps Slim went through when he started the thing. Tension hung in the frozen air like ... I don't know what, but we were all tense and nervous—all of us but Little Alfred, and he didn't seem worried at all.

He studied the controls, the gear shift, and so forth. Then he spied the key. His eyes brightened. "I think . . . I think you're 'posed to turn the key, and that'll start the motor."

Yes, but that was Step Two. Step One called for the driver to push in the clutch, and Alfred's legs were so short, they couldn't even reach the clutch, much less push it to the . . .

He turned the key.

The pickup lurched forward.

Holy smokes, he'd managed to start the dadgum pickup while it was in gear, and we were moving!

All the brightness went out of Alfred's face when he realized what he'd done. His eyes became big white saucers and he said, "Uh-oh, I think we're going to have a weck!"

He was right about that.

We Go Out into the Storm to Rescue Miss Viola

We were moving. Drover and I sat there like frozen statuaries, staring ahead at the swirling white void that lay just beyond the windshield. Alfred gripped the wheel. We were heading toward the edge of the little hill that sloped down to the yard.

Maybe he tried to turn, or maybe he saw what was coming and froze with fear, but he didn't make the turn. We chugged forward, came to the lip of the hill, started down, picked up speed, and . . . good grief, we were heading straight toward the . . .

CRUNCH!

Fence. We came to a sudden stop. Drover and I were thrown to the floor and ended up in a pile of legs and tails. We scrambled our respective legs around and managed to get ourselves properly aligned, but not before Drover kicked me on the nose. Twice.

"Would you stop kicking me on the nose?"

"Well, I'm just trying . . . we had a wreck!"

"I'm aware of that, but a wreck doesn't give you license to kick and paw the Head of Ranch Security on the nose."

At last I struggled to a sitting position and saw that we had just rammed the pickup into the fence around Sally May's yard and had laid a section of it flat on the ground. That was bad enough, but we were lucky the pickup had died in the process. Otherwise we might have driven right into the bedroom where Slim . . .

Huh?

Uh-oh. Speaking of Slim, guess who stepped out on the porch at that very moment. Yikes. He had looked sweeter and nicer when I'd thought he was a Mummy Monster. He surveyed the damage, shook his head, and motioned us into the house. I turned my eyes to Little Alfred. He was still gripping the steering wheel and had a sick look on his face.

"Oops. I wondoo what I did wong? I guess you're 'posed to push in the cwutch before you turn on the key."

Right. And I had tried to warn him about that.

"Welp, I guess we're in twouble again. Swim wooks mad, and when my mom gets home . . ." He made a scary face.

I began rehearsing my alibi. "Sally May, I know this looks pretty bad, I mean the fence knocked down and the, uh, honey tracks in the kitchen and . . . yes, the flour all over the . . . I realize it appears that we spent most of our time, uh, goofing off and engaging in, well, riotous behavior, but I think I can explain everything."

That's as far as I got. The terrible truth was that I couldn't explain everything. I couldn't explain any of it, except to say that . . . well, one thing had led to another.

And, yes, we were in twouble again.

Alfred opened the pickup door and we trooped into the house. Slim was waiting there in the utility room, towering above us like a huge tree with his arms crossed. Okay, maybe trees don't have arms, but he was derned sure towering and his arms were crossed and his puffy red eyes made him look pretty scary.

Drover and I went straight to the rug and

dropped like rocks and assumed the Pose of
Sleeping Dogs. Maybe he'd think we'd been there
all along. Yes, that was it. We'd been there on the
rug all along, good dogs to the end, and we knew
nothing, almost nothing at all about the . . . uh . . .
the crisis involving the pickup and the, uh, fence.

That had been Little Alfred's deal. We dogs
had been sleeping away, and then suddenly we'd
heard this crash, this loud crash, and we'd raised
our heads and . . . well, that had been our first
indication that something . . .

His gaze burned us up. I felt his eyes on me. I
squirmed and cringed and melted into a puddle of
hair. At last I dared to lift my head and give him
a limp cowdog smile that struggled to say, "Oh.
Hi there. We just woke up and . . ."

"You knotheads. Do you see what y'all have
done to the dadgum fence? What were you trying
to do out there?"

Alfred hung his head and pooched out his lips.
A tear slid down his cheek. "We were diss twying to
help, Swim. You were sick, so me and my doggies
were going to find Miss Viowa. I didn't mean to . . ."

That did it. He broke down and started bawl-
ing. Slim watched in silence as tears rolled off the
boy's cheeks and splattered on the floor. I noticed
that . . . hmm, the ice in Slim's eyes began to melt

just a bit. He looked away and shifted his weight
to the other leg. He swallowed, causing his Adam's
apple to hop around.

Alfred must have noticed too, because he
turned up the volume and spilled some more tears.
I saw an opening here and began tapping out the
rhythm of "We'll Never Pull This Stunt Again"
with my tail, and began beaming Sincere Mourn-
ful Looks in his direction. Have we ever done that
song? Maybe not. Here's how it went.

We'll Never Pull This Stunt Again

Hey Slim, we know we really goofed up
    badly.
Our hearts are broken beyond repair.
And now all three of us are feeling sadly.
That's why we're hiding beneath this chair.

We understand how bad this looks,
We're feeling like three common crooks,
We only wanted to impress
And help a lady in distress.

And yeah, okay, we know we should have
    waited
For you to come out and lend a hand.

And now the fence is flat, we really hate it.
We're feeling smaller than grains of sand.

The damage is already done,
We'd better hide his mother's gun.
Or maybe you could don your clothes
And fix the fence so no one knows?

Okay, it's time for Tragic Looks and pleading.
We beg forgiveness for our sin.
So be assured our broken hearts are bleeding.
We'll never pull this stunt again.

You think we're kidding?
No, we'll never pull this crazy stunt again.

By George, it was working! Before our very
eyes, Slim's flint heart began to soften, and he
said, "You knotheads. It was my bad luck to get
sick in a house with the Three Stooges. Okay, I'll
pull on some clothes and we'll see if we can find
Viola. I just hope I can stay awake to drive. I
think I've got Ensleepalosis."

Alfred stopped crying. "I can dwive."

"Sure you can. We just seen a prime example
of your driving skills, and I ain't impressed."

He beamed us one last glare and went off to the

bedroom, muttering under his breath. We waited. He didn't return. Five minutes passed, ten minutes. Alfred began to fidget, then he motioned for me to follow him and we went creeping through the house to see what was going on.

We passed through the ... arg, through the kitchen, and somebody sure needed to get that place cleaned up. It looked even worse than I remembered. We hurried through the kitchen and entered the darkened living room ... and there was Slim, sitting in the chair ... asleep! It appeared that he had sat down to pull on his boots, had gotten one pulled on, and had fallen asleep.

Well, that was a heck of a way to start a rescue mission.

Alfred tugged on his arm and woke him up. He blinked his puffy eyes and glanced around the room, then mumbled, "I'll be derned. Must have dozed off."

He finished pulling on his boots, put on his heavy coat and wool cap, and we were ready to brave the howling storm and rescue the lady in distress. We tromped through the house, gathered Mister Shivers from the utility room, and went out into the storm.

When we reached the pickup, Slim studied the damaged fence. He didn't say anything, but he gave us a glare that would have wilted a vase of flowers.

He wasn't real proud of us, it seemed.

He locked in the front hubs, which activated the four-wheel drive, and checked to be sure he had a tow chain on the back of the pickup. Then he opened the door and the three of us loaded up and sat on the cold seat, which was VERY COLD.

We shivered and breathed clouds of fog. Slim cut his eyes at us. "Y'all are fogging up the windshield. Reckon you could quit breathing for half an hour or so?"

Well, just what did he think . . . okay, he was joking. He smiled. With these cowboys, you never know. Sometimes they come up with bonehead ideas and they're serious.

He started the motor, wiped off the windshield with the back of his glove, put the pickup in reverse, and said, "Well, let's see if we can back out of your momma's yard." He gunned the motor, popped the clutch, and we plowed our way back up the hill. Then he put her in first gear and we drove around the north side the the machine shed, past the shelter belt, and on north toward the county road.

The north-south roads had blown clear of snow, but when we reached the county road and turned east, we found it pretty well drifted over. Slim turned on the windshield wipers and squinted at the road ahead.

"Boy, this is a nasty little storm. You sure don't expect this kind of snow so early in the year." He turned to Alfred. "If I know your daddy, I'll bet he's about to go nuts, listening to the weather report on the radio and walking the floor." His brow furrowed and he lifted his nose. "Somebody in this pickup stinks."

"It's my doggies. They got wet fwom the snow."

"You sure it ain't you?"

"It's not me, pwomise."

"Well, okay. But just in case, you'd better take a bath before your momma comes home. By the way, how did it happen that them dogs ended up inside the house?"

Alfred rolled his eyes. "Well, it was cold outside and I guess they just . . . came in."

"Uh-huh. Well, if we should happen to make it back to the house alive, it might be all right for them dogs to . . ."

You won't believe what happened next. All of a sudden . . .

He fell asleep!

Right in the middle of a sentence, Slim fell asleep at the wheel!

His chin fell down on his chest and the pickup began drifting toward the ditch—or what *used to be* the ditch. Now it was a big snowdrift. I happened to be looking at him when his lights went out and I saw a crisis-in-the-making in the making.

What did I do? I barked. Yes sir, I issued a loud clear bark to sound the alarm. It had no effect. He appeared to be in a deep measle-sleep. But I managed to get Alfred's attention. He gave me a puzzled look, then glanced at Slim and saw what had happened—we were heading straight for a big snowdrift in the north ditch!

CHAPTER ELEVEN

We Save Miss Viola from the Storm

Alfred responded at once and his response had the right effect. You know what he did? He screamed, and we're talking about a LOUD blurd-cuddling screech that rattled the windows—blood-curdling screech, I should say—and it was so loud, it hurt my ears.

It worked. Slim's eyes snapped open. He stared at the boy for a few seconds, then saw that we were heading for the ditch. He jerked the wheel at the very last moment and got us back into the road.

"I wasn't asleep," Slim muttered. "But you might better keep a watch out, just in case. Boy, these childhood diseases are sure hard on us grown men."

He gave his head a shake, blinked his eyes, and concentrated on the road ahead—of which there wasn't a whole lot to see, since the wind was driving the snow across it in ribbons and sheets and clouds. It had a kind of hypno . . . hypnomatic effect on all of us, even me. I mean, one second you could see the road, and the next it was gone, swallowed up in a big white blur. It made us all feel kind of dreamy.

But Little Alfred was on the job and he kept a sharp eye on Slim. Every time Slim's eyes started to glaze over, Alfred let out another screech. It worked, but Slim felt the need to grumble and complain about it.

"I hope my insurance covers ear damage. It wouldn't hurt my feelings if you screeched just a little softer."

"Yeah, but then you'd fall asweep and we'd get stuck in a snowdwift."

"Okay, but when you see me wearing hearing aids in both ears, you just remember who caused it."

Alfred laughed. "Oh Swim, you're funny."

"Great. I always wanted to be funny in the middle of a snowstorm. I sure hope we . . ." His voice trailed off, and I thought maybe he'd fallen asleep again, but then he said, "By netties, there she is."

All eyes turned toward the front. There in the

north ditch, was Viola's daddy's blue Ford pickup, high-centered and stuck in a snowdrift. We pulled up beside it and Slim rolled down his window. Viola rolled hers down too, and we could see her pretty face. Her cheeks were red from the cold and she wore a bright smile. Oh, and she had a fur cap on her head.

"Hi, boys. I guess I'm stuck."

I had a feeling that most of her smile was meant for . . . well, for ME, you might say, and I rushed over to the window to give her my warmest greeting. I mean, Miss Viola was my very most favorite lady friend and . . . okay, maybe I forgot about Slim sitting there when I rushed to the window and I guess my tail whacked him on the face and, well, knocked his glasses down on his nose. And maybe my hair was a little wet, but he sure didn't need to . . .

"Hank, for crying in the bucket, will you get away from me?" He shoved me back on the other side and fixed his glasses. "I know which one of us stinks now." He turned to Viola again. "I tried to tell you not to come."

"I know you did, Slim, but I don't always listen to you."

"Uh-huh, I noticed."

"How do you feel? You look terrible."

"Thanks. Looks tell it all, I reckon."

"Well, you don't have any business being out in this storm. Do you want to try to pull me out?"

Slim gave that some thought. "Don't think so. I just don't have any strength, Viola. I'm as weak as a poisoned pup, and I keep falling asleep. Why don't you get in and drive this thing? We'll pull you out when the storm breaks. By then, I'll either feel better or be dead." He turned to us dogs. "Now, I'm fixing to move myself over to the shotgun side, and any dogs that don't get out of the way are going to get smashed."

Okay, fine. Gee whiz, he didn't need to... Drover and I moved ourselves down to the floor and cleared the seat for Slim, while Miss Viola climbed in on the driver's side. Slim slid across, slumped against the door, closed his eyes, and laid his head against the window.

"Try not to get stuck this time. If you do, just open the door and roll me into the ditch and leave me for the coyotes." And with that, he was asleep.

Viola got in and sat behind the wheel. She found a place where she could turn around without getting stuck, and we made the long slow drive back to the house. Several times, she had to stop in the middle of the road. The snow was blowing so badly, she couldn't even see the hood of the pickup. The snow appeared to have stopped falling from the sky by then, and in fact we could see the sun popping through every once in a while, but the wind continued to blow the snow that had already fallen.

There's a name for this, by the way. It's called a "ground blizzard." You're probably amazed that I knew that, and maybe you wonder how I knew. Easy. Viola called it that.

It must have taken us ten or fifteen minutes to make it back to the house. Viola kept the pickup in second gear and crept along, following the tracks we had made in the snow, and at last we arrived at headquarters. She parked the pickup beside the yard gate and turned off the motor.

She beamed us a smile, her glorious bright sunshine smile, and said, "Well! That was fun, wasn't it." Then she tried to wake up The Measled Cowboy by calling his name. It didn't work. Alfred tried too, and got the same response—nothing. It appeared that I needed to step in and take charged of this deal, so I hopped up on the seat and went right to work licking Slim on the face and left ear.

After a few juicy licks, his eyes slid open. He cut them from side to side, then turned his head enough so that he could see me. His eyes were bloodshot and looked none too friendly, and in a

croaky voice he said, "Hank, if you don't quit licking me, I might be forced to pull your tongue out
by the roots and feed it to the buzzards. Quit." He
pushed me away and sat up. "Well, I reckon we
survived the trip. Nice work, Viola. I don't know
what you would have done without me."

That was a joke, I guess, and Miss Viola was
kind enough to laugh at it. "I'm sorry to cause you
all this trouble. You were right about the road. I
shouldn't have tried it but I did, and now I'm
here. Can you walk to the house?"

"Heck yes, I ain't an invalid. One more little
nap'll bring me around."

We all climbed out of the pickup and started
toward the back door. I noticed that Viola's gaze
fell upon the broken fence. "Should I ask what
happened to the fence?"

"Wind must have blowed it down," said Slim.

Her brows rose. "That must have been quite a
wind. It even left tracks in the snow."

Heh. Old Viola was ranch-raised and she'd
been taught to notice tracks. It wasn't easy to fool
her, and Slim didn't.

We made it to the back door. Slim stamped the
snow off his boots and opened the door. "Button, I
think the time has come to let them dogs . . ."
Zoom! In the twinkling of an eyeball, Drover and

I squirted through door. By the time Slim figured out what was happening, we had taken our positions on the rug in the utility room, had curled up into little furry balls, and were looking as innocent as dogs could possibly look.

I mean, the utility room needed guarding, right? And we had a lady visiting us and we sure as thunder didn't want to risk . . . something. You never knew what manner of stranger or monster might try to break into the house and . . .

Slim's eyes narrowed into cruel slits. Without lifting my head off the rug, I rolled my eye so that I could meet his gaze. In my deepest secret heart, I knew that we were fixing to be tossed out into the snow. He opened his mouth to speak, but just then . . .

The phone rang.

Slim's eyes blanked out. "Now, who could be calling at a time like this? I hope it ain't who I think it is." He went into the kitchen. His face was tense when he put the phone to his ear, but then it showed relief. "Why yes, howdy. Yep, she made it." He covered the phone and winked at Viola. "It's your daddy. No, all's well. Have you heard any weather? Good, good. I hope so. It was kind of a nasty little storm. Yes sir, we'll keep in touch. Bye."

He hung up the phone and heaved a sigh. "Boy, that was lucky. There for a second I thought it might be Loper or Sally May, calling to find out . . ."

By then, Viola had wandered into the kitchen. A look of horror filled her eyes. "What on earth happened in here?"

Slim dug his hands into his pockets and looked up at the ceiling. "Two dogs and one little boy, is all I can tell you."

She blinked several times. "Oh my. Sally May is going to . . ."

The phone rang again. Slim swallowed hard. "Uh-oh, I sure hope this ain't . . ." He wrapped his hand around the phone and put it to his ear. "Hello. Yes. Yes. Who? Well, I'll be derned. Hello, Sally May."

CHAPTER TWELVE

A Happy Ending, but Just Barely

The whole house fell silent. All eyes and ears went to Slim, whose face had suddenly turned as pale as oatmeal. From my position in the utility room, I strained to hear every word of the conversation.

"Yes, we had a little snow, we sure did, but tell Loper . . . he's been listening to the weather report, huh? I had a feeling he would, but tell him . . . no, the wind's blowing but the snow's quit, and y'all don't need to . . . you are? YOU ARE?" His eyes rolled up into his head. "Huh? No, no, everything around here is . . . normal. No problem. Yes ma'am, he's fine, been a perfect little . . . lad. No, them measles haven't bothered him at'all. Yalp. Okay. Bye."

He hung up the phone and slumped against the wall. "I knew it. They got as far as Anson and derned Loper heard we was having a storm. They've turned around and they're coming back like a horse to the barn. They'll be here soon."

An awful silence spread through the house, as each of us tried to imagine . . . gulp. Slim broke the silence.

"Viola, I don't know how this house got in such a state . . . well, yes I do, and I know who's going to get blamed for it too. I was a-wondering . . . what are the chances that a guy could hire you to do a little cleanup work?"

"A *little* cleanup?"

"Okay, a whole bunch. I ain't a wealthy man, but you could pretty well name your price."

A sly smile twitched at her mouth. She cocked her head and studied him for a moment. "I'll tell you what, Slim Chance, I'll bail you out of this wreck—on one condition."

"Go ahead, I'm at your mercy. Take anything but my saddle."

"Frankie McWhorter is going to play a dance in Twitchell this Saturday night. I'd just love to go."

"Uh-huh, and if I could dance, I'd just love to take you."

"That's my price."

"I dance like a cow on skates."

"You can learn."

"You're a hard woman, Viola, hard and mean and cruel."

"Take it or leave it."

He swallowed. "I think I'll take it."

"Good! I can hardly wait. Now, you go back to bed." Slim lifted one finger in farewell and departed for his sickbed. Viola removed her coat and hat and hung them up in the closet. "All right, Alfred, let's get started on..." She knelt down and studied something on the floor. "Is this... honey? And flour?" He gave his head a solemn nod. "Oh boy. I may have priced myself too cheap on this job. Well, let's get to work. We'll need buckets of hot water for this—hot water and elbow grease."

She found a plastic bucket and started filling it with hot water and soap. She pulled some rags and sponges out of the cabinet under the sink.

Alfred watched. "What's ebbow gwease?"

"You're fixing to learn, young man." She pitched him a rag. "Elbow grease means 'scrubbing,' lots of hard scrubbing."

He made a sour face. "My mom thinks I'm not old enough to help cwean house."

"Does she? Well, she'll be so surprised. Down

117

on the floor, son. Scrub. All that honey has to be wiped up or you'll have ants. Where does your mother keep the vacuum sweeper? Never mind. The power's still off. Okay, where does she keep the broom and dustpan?" Alfred pointed to the pantry. "I'll start sweeping up the flour and . . ."

She parked her hands on her waist and looked down at the boy. "How did this happen? And where was Slim? I mean, is it possible that a grown man could . . ." She swiped her hand through the air. "Never mind. Men. Down on your hands and knees and scrub."

Alfred thought he was too young to scrub counters and mop floors? Heh. He sure got proved wrong on that. He didn't work cheerfully, but under Miss Viola's stern gaze, he *did* learn to scrub and mop. It went on for hours, and it involved many fresh buckets of hot soapy water.

Drover and I observed it all from our position in the utility room. Well, actually I observed it all. Drover slept—and grunted and whistled and wheezed and contributed nothing. I observed and . . . well, felt a few moments of guilt. If I couldn't actually help clean up the mess I had, uh, helped create, at least I could show a few signs of guilt and remorse and so forth.

I did that, and you know what? It was a pretty

good deal. Showing a little remorse beats the heck out of scrubbing floors. Heh, heh. I'll take it every time.

Well, along about four o'clock in the evening they finished cleaning up the kitchen. By then, the sun was shining, the snow had started to melt, and the wind had died down. The storm had blown itself out, and it was hard to believe that only hours before, we had been in the grisp of the grasp of a howling blizzard. That's Panhandle weather for you.

Anyways, along about four they finished the so forth and Viola put away all the cleaning supplies. It was amazing, what she'd been able to do. The house, which had seemed unfixable and uncleanable only hours before, was now restored to its previous condition. I was impressed.

Viola leaned against the counter and removed the bandana she had tied around her head. She seemed satisfied . . . but she wasn't finished.

"Alfred, it's time to wake up Slim. We've got one more job to do, and not much daylight left." When Alfred protested that he was worn out, she smiled. "Cleaning up these messes isn't as much fun as making them, is it? Now you know what your mother goes through every day."

Alfred pooched out his lip. "Well, it was Hank

that made most of the mess, and he didn't have to cwean up anything."

"I'll bet. Go wake up Slim. We've got to fix that piece of yard fence . . . that the wind blew down."

Alfred flashed her a devilish grin. "It wasn't the wind. I dwove the pickup into it, but don't tell my mom."

"No, really? I never would have guessed it was you."

Alfred went to fetch Slim, and Viola turned her . . . boy, she had the prettiest brown eyes I'd ever seen, and when she turned them on me, I just melted. What a fine gal! She understood dogs, she liked dogs, she . . .

"Boys, I hate to tell you this, but it's time for y'all to move out. I don't think Sally May would approve." Alfred and Slim appeared just then, and Viola aimed a finger at the boy. "Alfred, I'm putting these dogs out. *Don't* let them back inside, and Slim Chance, don't you let them in either. This house is clean and I want it to stay that way."

Slim nodded. "Yes ma'am. Don't worry about me."

"I worry about both of you, all four of you. One's just as bad as the others. Now, what do we need to fix the fence?"

Slim scratched the top of his head. "Well . . .

posthole diggers, hammer, tamping bar, shovel, some steeples, wire stretchers, a couple of fresh posts. Sure sounds like a lot of trouble, don't it."

"Yes. Let's get on with it."

Slim muttered and shook his head and went slouching toward the back door. "You're a heartless woman, Viola, and you dogs are officially banished from the house—forever. Out!" He pushed open the door and jerked his head toward the outside. Drover and I made a dash out the door. As I flew past, Slim gave me a kick to the tail section and said, "You birdbrains."

Was that necessary? Hey, I was trying to . . . oh well. Sticks and stones may break my bones, but I was still Miss Viola's very favorite dog. So there.

Well, once we were done with all the kicks and insults, we flew into the task of repairing the fence. Miss Viola was there to supervise, so this wasn't a typical Slim Chance Repair Job. She made him fix it *right*, so that when Sally May drove up, she wouldn't notice that the fence had been repaired. That was pretty smart.

Oh, and you know what else she made Slim do? She made him get a shovel and fill in the muddy tracks that led down to the fence—fill 'em in, smooth 'em out, and cover 'em up with snow!

Old Slim howled at that—howled and griped and complained every step of the way. But when he was done, he leaned on the shovel, looked it over, and admitted that she'd been right. Well, that was progress.

By the time Slim had put up all the tools and stuff, it was after five o'clock. We all hopped into the pickup and drove over to Miss Viola's pickup and pulled it out of the snowdrift. Slim thanked her for saving our lives, and then he promised to make good on his deal—to take her to Frankie's dance on Saturday night. And then we all said our good-byes and she drove off. Watching her leave, we all felt . . . well, a little sting of sadness.

And Slim said, "Boys, that's a pretty fine gal right there."

Yes, she certainly was, but there was something Slim didn't know about, and something I would never tell him. When she left, Miss Viola gave ME an extra special smile and wink. I was pretty sure she wanted me to go to the dance with them. Why not? Heck, I figured I could dance as well as Slim.

But just then, we heard the hum of a car motor in the distance, and that brought our thoughts back to earth. Slim turned the pickup around and we met Loper and Sally May just as they reached the mailbox. Slim pulled up beside them and rolled down his window.

Loper studied our faces. "What's up?"

"Oh, nuthin' much. We were just checkin' out the snow."

"It wasn't as bad as the radio said."

"Nope."

"Alfred feeling okay?"

"Yalp."

"Any wrecks or disasters?"

"Nope."

Loper scanned our faces. We held our breaths. "Huh. That's a miracle. Well, I guess we could have gone on to Abilene."

"Yalp, but that wouldn't be you."

"What's wrong with your face? It's all red and you look awful."

"Thanks. Your kid gave me the measles."

"Huh. Sorry. You want to come up to the house for supper?"

"No thanks. I'm going home to bed. If I don't show up in two weeks, call the undertaker."

Loper laughed. "I'll check on you in the morning. Sleep's the best medicine." Loper studied us with questioning eyes. "Is there more to this story?"

"Yalp, but you ain't going to hear it today. Maybe next week. Or next month."

And that was about it. Alfred jumped into the car with his folks and they drove down to the house. We turned around and headed for Slim's shack. As we chugged along the Wolf Creek Road, Slim let out a big breath of air and gave us dogs a grin.

"Well, boys, we dodged a bullet on this deal."

Yes, thanks to Miss Viola, we had dodged a major bullet. Sally May didn't hear the full story until two days later, and by then . . . well, it was already too late to kill us, and all she could do was laugh and shake her head.

Case closed.

And Miss Viola really was crazy about me, no kidding.

Have you read all of Hank's adventures?

More Security Force Benefits

- Special discounts on Hank books and audiotapes
- An original Hank poster (19" x 25") absolutely free

For more information write to:

Hank's Security Force
Maverick Books
PO Box 549
Perryton, Texas 79070

John R. Erickson

began writing stories in 1967 while working full-time as a cowboy, farmhand, and ranch manager in Texas and Oklahoma—where two of the dogs were Hank and his sidekick Drover. Hank the Cowdog made his debut a long time ago in the pages of *The Cattleman*, a magazine about cattle for adults. Soon after, Erickson began receiving "Dear Hank" letters and realized that many of his eager fans were children.

The Hank the Cowdog series won Erickson a *Publishers Weekly* "Listen Up" Award for Best Humor in Audio. He also received an Audie from the Audio Publishers Association for Outstanding Children's Series.

The author of more than thirty-five books, Erickson lives with his wife, Kris, and their three children on a ranch near his boyhood home of Perryton, Texas.